Promise of Judith

BY TOY TAYLOR
PRINTED IN THE U.S.A

PRINTED ISBN: 978-1-7330606-0-8

EBOOK ISBN: 978-1-7330606-1-5

PUBLISHED BY: TOY TAYLOR

PUBLICATION: MAY 2019

Promise of Judith
Book II
Toy Taylor

5

The decisions we make before we have them, even effect our kids.

Toy

TABLE OF CONTENTS

Introduction

We watched Edith maneuver her way through various events that could have left her stunted and depressed. Despite taking life changing blows, she kept her mind at peace. Most teenagers that experience trauma at their most impressionable ages have damaging residual effects. The juvenile detention centers around the world are full of children that act subconsciously in pain.

Everyone is not built to withstand the throes of life. Especially not our kids. Edith was not a robot. She had feelings and she expressed emotion, but not to detrimental levels.

She was under the impression that her troubles started with the overdose of her father. The truth is, her troubles were the residual effects of her parents buried past. Pieces she thought had just began to move in her life were actually owed for the emotional debt her parents were in. She realizes her own origins were all a portrait painted by her mother and father as her life unravels.

Would her parents have made different choices if they could have predicted the consequences? Would her life had been better if they had done what society proclaims is "the right thing"? Who is to say they were not convinced they were doing the right thing? Time is the best story teller. It will keep the spoilers to itself and taunt the characters.

We walked away from Edith with so many unknowns. Throughout her story, her mother in particular made unapologetic decisions. These decisions seemed to have a motivation only known to herself. Edith is very clear herself about her mother's understood privacy throughout the story.

This leaves the reader to wonder, "privacy for what"? Why would someone who holds everyone accountable need so much privacy. They should be holding themselves to the same standard right? Not hardly. We will see this as the story of Judith unfolds.

Judith herself is a residual effect of Edith's existence. Their mom made decisions that would cause both of them to experience life changes at impressionable times. Cheri's love for her girls is obvious. She takes good care of them despite her feelings or the trauma going on around them.

It is just a shame that her decisions are seemingly causing the most trauma. Things happen. People get sick. People lose jobs. Sometimes the economy will take a family or business down.

She made deliberate choices that affected her children. She had the opportunity to make decisions that would have had less aftershocks. Her decisions only add to the trauma that life promises anyone who lives. Her socioeconomic status does not take away from her failure to make less selfish decisions.

Cheri will show us what it means to have too much control. She prides herself on making sure it looks all together. She is not the only mother guilty of this. We saw during Edith's story that she was held responsible for all the emotional debt she owed. What she thought was holding everything together, was setting the stage to rip everything she will build a part.

Her children are involuntary riding an emotional rollercoaster. The owner of the theme park is Cheri. Edith gave us a chance to see her mother face up with her decisions. The Promise of Judith will show us the real circumstances surrounding her decisions. The reader can be the judge of The Judge's motives.

The reader is also responsible for evaluating themselves as well. What are your motives for your decisions in Life? How will they affect your children? What possible damage will your decision do to your generations.

There is this thing called "generational curses". As the author, I call them destructive propensities that have been accepted for generations. I believe many of these so called curses would be broken if a few in the family would ban together and commit to generational healing. Most people are too caught up in their own careers and well being to do that.

Many parents make brash decisions knowing the decision will call for an apology later. Some parents fail to even apologize. This makes the behavior acceptable to a child that will emulate the behavior in spite or instinctually. Just like Edith, many kids do not even realize their bad decisions are rooted deeper than them.

Chapter 1: A Stranger Did It

"Hey yo! Hurry up doll face. I do not have all night. Especially for a girl not mine." John Paul was yelling at Cheri as she walked down the steps of her parent's porch.

Cheri did not flinch. She did not react or respond to John Paul's rantings. She was used to it. They were old high school buddies. He always gave her a hard time about not dating him. She had her reasons though.

John Paul was an arrogant jock that led a privileged life. Many of the girls in their high school were after him because of his athletic status. They had good reason to be. He had been a varsity starter since his freshman year. He was highly recruited before he started his senior year.

Cheri did what few girls did. Every time he propositioned her to exclusively date, she told him "no". She would accept sporadic invitations to hang out and grab a bite of food. She was home from law school for the summer. Tonight, was one of those sporadic nights.

She climbed gracefully into his luxury two-seater. After getting his degree in sports administration, John Paul was running a sports talent agency and recruiting firm. His ego was evidently bigger than before.

"Dang woman, it is about time." He snarled as she closed the car door.

"Look, you had every opportunity to drive away. You did not. You waited. Learn to wait patiently." Cheri finally snapped back.

"Oh, I have much patience. We both are very aware of what I am waiting for." He said this time matter of factly.

"Enlighten me my friend." Cheri inquired.

"See there you go. Calling me friend. I know we are friends. You also know how I feel about you. You know I want to be more than that." He softened his tone to signal he was serious.

"You also have a girlfriend at home. I pay attention every time a number calls you unsaved in your phone. So, you feel exactly what for me?" She replied.

"You think I would not dead all of that to make sure you are happy. You have never given me a chance. I just want someone worth my love before I give it away." John Paul was very sincere it seemed.

Cheri sighed. "Look I live in New York. I just do not have an interest in a long-distance relationship. I have a big enough load and burden as I try to finish up law school. You know how important this is to me." She tried not to let him down hard.

He did not respond immediately. He rubbed his forehead with his index and his thumb as if he was thinking. Then he said, "That is why I want to spend my life with you. I am sure of it. Promise me you will give me a chance if the timing is right."

She knew very well she did not mean it, but she said, "I promise."

The two enjoyed each other the rest of the night. They always did. They had great chemistry as friends. Cheri's mother always hoped she would end up with John Paul. When he came around, she called him her "son in law".

John Paul was a gentleman to her all night as he always was. He opened her car door when they stopped. They went to a local bar to watch a game and have a few drinks. It was their usual.

They both enjoyed sports and had participated in organized sports most of their lives. As the night ended, John Paul did something out of the ordinary. He asked Cheri could they stop at a popular couple spot in town just to talk. He mentioned he wanted to spend a little more time before she flew back to New York.

She had known John Paul for years. She trusted him to just talk and take her safely home. He had seen her home safely for years. "Sure, I do not have big plans tomorrow," she said agreeing.

He took her to "Lovers Leap". It was a spot that earned its name because a chilling history. The spot was up on a high cliff overlooking their town. There were a few cars there before they arrived.

John Paul parked his car and sat staring out towards the town lights. He did not seem to have much to talk about once they arrived. His phone vibrated a few times upon their arrival. He ignored the calls and it seemed like he was ignoring Cheri.
"You ok?" She asked noticing he was in deep thought.

"Yea, I just. I do not want to say the wrong thing. Look, it has been over ten years since we met right?" He as incredulously.

"I guess so. We met as high school freshman, and a few degrees later, I guess a decade has passed." Cheri chose her words. She was not sure where John Paul was going with his questioning.

"Have I ever failed to show you loyalty and respect?" He continued.

"No." She responded. She felt the questions pushing her into another "Why not me speech?".

"Look, I'm tired of this. I cannot help how I feel. I feel like you are stringing me along. Especially if you know how I feel about you." He began to sound agitated.

His energy was well received, but not accepted. "Stringing you along? We talk all the time. We always have as friends. I am very clear about my status in your life. I am on purpose so that you cannot make the accusations that you are now." She was becoming irritated herself.

"Take me home." She demanded.

"No." He smirked.

"What?" Cheri was ready to storm from his car. She had nowhere to storm to. She was far from home. It would have been too unsafe to try and walk or hitch a ride.

"Look, you either are going to let me try it. Or you can figure out how to get home. I have done less for panties. It is time you know who you are dealing with." John Paul projected a persona she had not seen. It was the persona he was rumored to have possess.

"I will find a way." Cheri grabbed for her purse and the car door handle. She would just stay in someone's sight and call one of her sisters.

John Paul grabbed her arm before she could get out. He pulled her back in and placed her hand on his lap. She repulsed back. He would not let go.

"Don't do this." Is all she could manage to get out before he grabbed the back of her neck.

He forced her to kiss him and tried to fondle her breast. Cheri began to fight him as her survival switch was flipped. The two tussled in his small vehicle for what seemed like an eternity. John Paul assured her he would get what he wanted no matter how much she fought.

Suddenly another couple knocked on the car window. They asked if everything was okay. When they realized Cheri was being attacked, they called the police. John Paul released his grip as the couple were making their 911 call.

He pushed Cheri out of his vehicle and sped away. The couple asked if she had anyone to call before the police arrived. John Paul had sped away with her purse and phone. Still, there were a few numbers she knew by heart.

"Hello" a sleepy voice said on the other end of her Samaritan phone call.

"Edwin, I am so sorry." Cheri began.

Noticing something was wrong he jumped from bed, "Hey what is wrong? Where are you?"

"Can you pick me up from Lovers Leap? I have to explain later." She said immediately.

"Sure, I will be there soon." Edwin began heading towards Cheri as soon as they hung up.

The police arrived before Edwin did. The couple that had aided her gave reports and a description of John Paul to the cops. When they tried to interview Cheri, she was very reluctant. She knew the cops knew who John Paul was and did not want the attention of the incident.

Instead of telling the truth about her attack, she led on as if they had just met. She trumped the assault up to be a night gone wrong with a badly chosen beau. She was clear she did not want to pursue charges despite her apparent injuries. She just wanted to make it home.

When Edwin arrived, they released Cheri into his custody. They strongly suggested that she was seen by a medical professional. They both agreed to get the cops to go. Cheri had not intention on seeing a doctor.

"What happened babe?" Edwin began his questioning as soon as they were alone. "Who were you with?"

"Ed, give me a second. Please." Cheri was shaken by the incident. The thoughts of what could have happened to her began to play in her head.

"No, who were you with. I know you were not just out with someone you do not know. I know you better than that. Who are you protecting?" Edwin pressed.

Cheri began to cry. Edwin was right. He did know her; he knew her very well. They had dated in high school. He was her first love. Their present predicament moved her to tears. She should have been with him.

Sensing he was applying too much pressure, Edwin backed off. He was not done though. He loved Cheri. It just seemed like timing was never right for them. He wanted to know who she was with, partly out of his own guilt.

He felt responsible for her. He would have rather they stayed together. Cheri insisted that she did not want a long-distance relationship because of school. She moved further from their home after she was awarded her first degree.

This prompted Edwin to move on from a girl who was never coming back. They saw each other during summer and holiday breaks. No matter how many times they talked, Cheri never eluded to coming home. Edwin was invested in his family businesses; he had no desire to leave home and follow her.

"Will you drop me off at a hotel? I need the night to clean up and think about what to tell my parents." Cheri finally asked breaking their silence.

"Sure".

Edwin found a nice hotel not far from his life. He wanted to be close if she needed him tonight or in the morning. He also saw that she was checked in and had comfortable accommodations. He notified the clerk to charge his business credit card for as many nights as Cheri needed.

When they entered the hotel room, he made sure it was empty. He checked all window and access door locks. He clearly cared about this woman and her safety. After everything was secure, he noticed she had jumped into the shower while he was occupied.

He waited for her to finish, as a gentleman does. Cheri appeared from the bathroom freshly showered and glowing. Edwin was glad that he had waited to tell her bye. The sight of his fist love in a bathrobe was worth his troubles.

"Hey, I thought you would have left me by now." Cheri said thinking he would have hurried home.

"I considered it, but I wanted to make sure you had all you needed before I left." Edwin told her with a smile.

He stood up to meet her as she came toward him. She naturally fell in his arms and rested for a few seconds. "What else you need babe?" He asked while they stood holding each other after a while. Cheri did not respond.

Edwin stepped back and gently grabbed her face. He kissed her nose. As he did this, a single tear rolled down her face. "What is It? Tell me." Edwin would do just about anything for her and she knew it.

Finally, Cheri found the courage to say something. "I want you Ed. I am so sorry. I know what I did to us. I just, I am sorry. Just go. I know you have to go." She buried her face in his chest.

He did have to go. They both knew he had to go. He decided to not leave right away however. "Let me stay with you for a little while. I miss you." He told her and without hesitation.

He grabbed her by her waist and led her towards the hotel bed. They laid down together and he stroked her back as she fell asleep. He had no idea she was going to call. He hated the circumstances surrounding the call. He was glad to see her.

He even had an idea of who she was out with. He simply decided to leave the matter alone until she was comfortable enough to talk about it. He was not sure what all had happened. He just hoped not the worst of his suspicions.

Edwin had planned on massaging Cheri until she fell asleep. While he massaged her, she began to massage him back. The two are entangled in their love before either of them could stop the boundaries that were being disrespected. Their loyalty to one another blinded them to their realities as always.

Edwin even tried to stop after he had entered her for the first time in a while. It was unsuccessful. The two made love as if they had never left each other's side. They had no regard for the morning because their love for each other veiled any obligation.

After releasing his energy multiple times, Edwin fell asleep with Cheri unintentionally. It was the sound of the shower and the morning sun that woke him up. He ran to jump in the shower with Cheri. When he looked at the time, he realized he would be late for cake tasting with his fiancé.

"You in a rush babe?" Cheri was glad he had joined her in the shower.

"Yea, I have a prior engagement. I already have to explain not going home. I want to make it to the cake tasting on time." Edwin explained while he showered quickly.

"Hey," Cheri demanded his attention.

"Yea babe?"

"Thanks for everything. I know I do not deserve it."

"Cheri, I will do anything for you. I just have to make it to this cake tasting on time. I can even see you after." Edwin said sensing the heaviness of them about to go separate ways.

"No, I have to get ready to fly out. I am going to head back early to start my last year. I am just grateful. I tried to respect your new fiancé. That is why I have not called all summer." She felt guilty for having to call on him as always.

"It is never a problem if I get to see you. You know that." Edwin returned to his quick shower.

Cheri did not want to make him even later for his obligations. She had one of her sisters pick her up before she checked out. She called her baby sister because she would ask the least amount of questions. She still did not know how she was going to explain missing all night and coming home with a busted lip.

She did not want to tell her family what John Paul had done. Whether they liked him or not, they would have pursued justice. Pursuing justice would have meant letting everyone know who she was with. Including her boyfriend back in New York; Kerry.

He was interning with highly accredited dental office in the city. She was finishing up her law degree. The last thing she needed was him finding out about John Paul. She definitely did not want him to get wind of Edwin, the love of her life. She figured the details of the night were better left unsaid.

Chapter 2: He is not the Dean, His Name is Dean

"Hello Beautiful." Kerry said greeting Cheri in the airport terminal.

"Hi you." She replied with a smile.

They did their usual hugs and kisses. This time Kerry took a bit longer. He was very excited to see his lover. He thought she was the best thing to happen to him besides his mother. He treated her like a queen.

This is what drew Cheri to him. She had a few beau's to compare to. Of them all, she loved the way Kerry treated her. He had always been a gentleman since they had met her first year of law school.

Kerry picked up her bags in one hand and grabbed her hand with his free hand. They were happy to see each other. Cheri loved Texas. It was easier to find work in New York. She had been a military brat and she lived in various locations. It was not foreign for her family to travel to see one another.

"How was your trip my love?" Kerry asked as they entered his vehicle.

"It was wonderful." She said smiling. It was a poker face. She internally cringed and was glad to be safe with Kerry.

"So, what did you do the last few days? I feel like we have not spoken much." He asked inquisitively.

"Let's see. I did a lot of packing. My mom made me spend my last moments with her. That just consisted of a lot of errands." Cheri did not know what to say. She hoped he would change the subject.

"Well are you ready to finish up this year?" He asked unintentionally granting her wish.

"Of course, I am. How are things with You? I did not have many missed calls from you either." She chimed.

"Aww you know. I am finishing up my internship. Since you weren't here, I hung out with the guys."

"Doing what?" She cut him off. Kerry was great. Kerry was far from perfect. They have had to make it through a few of his struggles.

"Love. Relax. I was not doing anything you would not approve of. Well, maybe my food choices." He said trying to sooth her.

His words did not make her any less suspicious. She just did not want to press. She had her own activities she had rather not discussed. She noticed he was not going toward their townhouse as she let the conversation go.

"Where are we going?" She asked.

"You hungry aren't you? I figured we grab a bite before going home. There is not much there. You look too exhausted to cook." He said grabbing her thigh.

"Thanks hunny." She sat back and relaxed while he drove.

She thought on his last comment. She thought to herself that is why she loved him. He was thoughtful and attentive. He took care of her better than she took care of herself sometimes. She was grateful to have him as a partner. This simultaneously made her feel guilty as well.

Her trip to Texas was an eye opener. Coming home and realizing what Kerry meant to her, gave her even more clarity. This clarity meant she had to clean some other things up. She could leave Texas in Texas. She had to fix somethings right there in New York.

School would start in a few days and she would have her chance. She could finally focus only on Kerry and their future after one more conversation. She just hoped that conversation did not affect her academic standing.

Kerry had ordered Italian without even asking. It was her favorite cuisine. He ordered takeout so they could hurry home and enjoy one another. After dinner they shared a shower and went promptly to bed. Kerry left for work early. Cheri was physically and emotionally fatigued.

The next few days flew by like a whirlwind. Cheri spent most of the time studying for the first day of class. Her program was highly competitive. She wanted to be up to speed with her counterparts who had probably dedicated their whole summer to law studies.

She also wanted to be prepared for Dean. He was not the Dean. He was a professor whose name happen to be Dean. They met her first year while he was just a assistant professor. He had since been promoted to a professor with tenure.

Their relationship was not forbidden. It was just she was in a relationship with Kerry. He surprised her with a proposal to be exclusive and she accepted without thought for Dean. She only saw him during the academic calendar.

The first day of school came faster than she thought. When she woke up, she had knots on her stomach that made her feel sick. She shook it off as her first day jitters and prepared for school. She knew her schedule would be light the first day. She planned to talk with Dean and get it over with. Kerry deserved that.

She found him in his office after her last scheduled course. He was pleased to see her, and she could tell. She just hoped he would take her news well. He was not the most understanding person she had met.

"You missed me?" He asked confidently.

Cheri did not want to lead him on. She went in with a purpose. She stuck to it. "Listen I need to talk to you." She said immediately.

"Oh, about?" He got serious sensing her tone.

"Us. I cannot continue with us. I just wanted to make that clear before school really got started." She said firmly.

"Hmmm. Why now?"

"That is my personal choice Dean."

"Ok. Let me ask you something." He rose from behind his desk to walk toward her. "Can I touch you just one more time?"

"No." She replied firmly.

"Hmmmm. Ok. Have a nice day." He said dismissively.

Cheri normally would have reacted. She refrained. She felt she should take the invitation to leave. If she would have responded to his tone, they would have ended up all over each other. He knew that when he dismissed her.

Feeling good about her decision and their future, she headed home to Kerry. The first day of her last year was almost over. She wanted to make him dinner and end the day on a good note. Maybe even on Kerry.

The first couple of weeks of school were as hard as she expected. As September approached, Cheri wanted to surprise Kerry with a anniversary celebration. Nothing too big. Just a quaint gathering to share the celebration with a few friends.

She called her best friends to help with some of her planning. She loved throwing gatherings. She in fact enjoyed preparing the foods and decor. The last couple of weeks had been unusually tough for her. She figured she was still getting back in the groove of school.

Rubi flew over to Cheri's townhouse faster than she could hang up the call. She loved Kerry and Cheri together. She was more than happy to make their night special. She and Cheri met in undergrad school. Cheri went on to pursue law studies and Rubi entered the engineering field.

"Thanks for coming over girl!" Cheri exclaimed as she welcomed her into her home.

"No problem, you know the guys went fishing so I was all by myself." Rubi explained.

"Well the universe worked it all out. I have been so tired lately. I need a little help planning our anniversary." Cheri replied.

"Well what do you have in mind?" Rubi asked.

"That is why you are here. I want to do something special. It is our third year. I have never really celebrated him. He always celebrates and surprises me." Thinking of Kerry's gestures made her heart smile.

"Why don't we have a seafood boil?" Rubi suggested.

"Na, that is a normal gathering."

"Well where? Home? At this point, you are our celebrity chef in the circle. If you make anything it will be a normal gathering." Rubi suggested.

"You are right. But where?" Cheri wondered.

"There is a new lounge that opened downtown while you were gone. I hear it is very chic. I bit on the expensive side though." Rubi offered.

"That could work. I will check it out on my way to school this week. Unless it is a half burned down shack, it will do. I trust you." Cheri answered as she got up to grab her vibrating phone.

It was Edwin. He had called a few times since she had been home. She decided not to answer yet. She wanted to find a way to tell him they should relax their ties. She was ready to fully be faithful to Kerry.

Rubi noticed that she put her phone back with hesitation. "Who was that?" She asked Cheri.

"Nobody girl, I thought I knew the number." She lied. No one in New York she associated with knew about Edwin. Not even the person she considered her closest friend.

"Ok well it sounds like we have parts of a plan. We can move forward once you check out the venue. I am going to make a stop before Greg comes home." Rubi said grabbing her things.

"I really appreciate you stopping by girl! I will call you once I check out the place. I am going to take a nap myself before Kerry comes." Cheri said readying to walk her out.

Cheri's phone continued to vibrate while she saw Rubi to the front door. She contemplated talking to Edwin while she was alone. She was just too afraid. She did not want to bear his reaction. Him being upset would be hard. Him not being upset would be hard. She loved that man, but he was someone else's fiancé.

She thought it best to nap before Kerry came in. She woke up early to do some weekend studying. She wanted to have energy for him when he came. She had also eaten a breakfast burrito that morning that was giving her unusual indigestion. She decided to rest that off too.

Her nap was cut short when Kerry arrived home. "You sleep again? It seems like all you do is sleep my beauty." He kissed her while he woke her up from her impromptu nap.

"You know how much I study. I have been up since 4am. I figured I would take a nap to rest up for you." Cheri said playing with Kerry's collar.

"Oh yeah?" Kerry said intrigued. "Rest of for what?"

"For whatever you need." She answered.

"That is what I like to hear." Kerry jumped on top of Cheri before she could respond.

She was still tired though she had a nap. She and Kerry loved each other until he was finished. She promptly showered and made dinner to start their evening. He tried to make small talk with her, but her responses left little room for conversation.

She was unintentionally being short with him. He figured she was just tired. He did wake her up from a nap. She was indeed tired. She was mostly engulfed in her own subconscious.

A part of her was preoccupied with Kerry's party plans. The other part was wondering what to tell Edwin. Neither part realized she was being short with Kerry. He knew her though. He figured something was on her mind.

Fall was becoming to take over New York and the rest of the country. She knew eventually she would have to go to Texas. She was weighing the benefits of cutting him off now or later. At least later she could do it in person. She still was stuck with the fact that she was currently ignoring him.

She had heard he had a beautiful wedding ceremony to open the fall. Her sister, who happens to be friends with the bride, also announced they were expecting a baby. Cheri expected the wedding. She was shocked Edwin had gotten her pregnant so fast. She felt he was taking many things fast with his new bride.

Chapter 3:
Happy
Anniversary!

"SURPRISE!" A small crowd shouted at 910 Bar and Lounge.

"Oh wow! Thank you guys!" shouted Kerry over the crowd and soft jazz music.

The place Rubi suggested was perfect. Cheri fell in love with it when she saw it. It had dim lights and soft jazz playing in the background. She felt the service was impressive before she was a paying customer.

After she booked the venue, she and Rubi worked hard to make plans without Kerry finding out. The hardest part was swearing his best friends to secrecy. They hid all the decorations and party accessories at Rubi's house. Kerry asked a lot of questions about going to a mystery location. He eventually played along.

"Happy Anniversary man!" Kerry's best friend said approaching him. "You lucky man, all I got for our anniversary was a list of chores!"

"Yea man, I have a special one," Kerry said glancing over at Cheri.

"Look I cannot stay long, but I wanted you to know I was here man." Jimmy said taking a shot.

"Yea right. Who are you going to stay with? I know you told your wife you would be here the whole time." Kerry inquired.

Jimmy did not dignify him with an answer. That gave Kerry all the evidence he needed to prove his assumption. He and Jimmy grew up together. Jimmy always used his events as a cover up to spend time with his side females. Kerry did not approve, but Jimmy was a grown man.

Cheri made her way over to Kerry once she saw Jimmy walk away. "He going to get some panties?" She whispered in his ear.

"Yea. Yet, he wonders why his marriage is not as solid as our relationship." Kerry added. "Thank you so much, I am lucky to have you my lady."

"Aww. You are welcome. Go enjoy yourself and your guest." Cheri said sending him away.

"Yes mam." Kerry said kissing her as they went in opposite directions of the lounge.

Cheri had to find Rubi. She woke up that morning feeling sick and faint. She thought it would wear off. It seemed as the day had progressed it had gotten worse. It was in full swing at the party. The smell of alcohol and foreign foods had made it worse.

"Hey Rubi." Cheri said grabbing her shoulder. She felt like she was going to faint.

When Rubi turned around, she was immediately alarmed. "You ok girl?"

"Not really can I talk to you?" Cheri said obviously mustering up strength.

They found a private spot in the lounge to talk. Cheri explained how she had been feeling all day. Rubi suggested she go to an Urgent Care facility. It sounded like Cheri had flu symptoms to her.

Cheri agreed with her. She decided to find Kerry and explain to him. She hoped it did not put too much of a damper on the night. They had worked really hard to make sure it was a success. Rubi was kind of bummed they had to leave. She did not want to send her friend alone though.

"Babe. I'm going to run to an Urgent Care." Cheri said when she found Kerry.

"Alright, let me tell a few people goodbye." He said immediately.

"No no no. Stay enjoy yourself. Rubi will go with me." Cheri cut him off.

"What? What is wrong?" He asked puzzled.

"I have been feeling bad all day. We are just going to make sure I do not have the flu." Cheri tried to sooth his obvious worry.

46

"Well I do not mind going with you babe."
He still said.

"I know, but I did all of this for you. I want you to enjoy yourself. I will meet you at home." Cheri said kissing him.

"Alright, will you call me if it is something serious?" He asked worried.

"I promise." She replied.

Cheri and Rubi headed to the nearest Urgent Care they could find. Lucky for her it was not packed. They were able to see a nurse almost immediately. The nurse asked one question that stopped Cheri in her tracks.

"What was the date of your last period?"

Cheri did not respond. She was shocked. She had four sisters; she knew a pregnant woman's symptoms. She had ignored all of her own.

The nurse repeated the question. "Mam what is the date of your last period?"

"Uh, I am a not sure. Before August." It was the last week of September. She had not had a period since she had been in New York.

"Based on your symptoms and information, I am going to start with a pregnancy test. Although it sounds like we do not need one." The nurse replied.

Cheri reluctantly took the pregnancy test. She was just as sure as the nurse that she was pregnant. The problem was, she was not prepared to be pregnant her last year of law school. She was terrified.

The results only took a few minutes. The nurse confirmed the positive pregnancy test. After, she suggested that Cheri schedule an appointment with her OBGYN as soon as possible. She told her to stay hydrated and eat healthy in the meantime. Her flu like symptoms were side effects of pregnancy.

Cheri contemplated telling Rubi as she waited for her discharge paperwork. She decided she wanted Kerry to be the first person she told. She told Rubi the nurse just suggested she get rest and follow up with her primary care doctor. She would save the secret as another surprise for Kerry that night.

She had fallen asleep before he returned home. He woke her up as always. "Hey sweetie. What did the doctor say? You better?" He inquired.

"Not really better, but I found out what was wrong." She said hesitantly. "Kerry I am pregnant."

"What?" Kerry jumped up from her side excited. He noticed she was not as excited as he was. "What's wrong?"

"You know I have already been struggling through school. I will have a newborn at the same time I am studying for the Bar Exam. That stresses me out Kerry." She said softly.

"Hey hey now. You have me. We can do this." He said stroking her hair. "I cannot promise it will be easy. We will get through it."

"Kerry, I love you. You just do not strike me as a diaper changing champion." Cheri said jokingly.

"You are right. I will become one for my baby though. Watch and see." He laughed as he touched her stomach.

The two of them spent the subsequent weeks accepting and deciding how to prepare for a new baby. They made changes to their budget. They changed their hours of rest to accommodate Kerry working more hours. He knew that Cheri's parents took care of her while she was in school. Neither of them knew what her parent's reaction would be to another mouth to feed.

He wanted to be prepared for no help. Even if he had to leave work himself to help the mother of his first child. Kerry was more excited than Cheri. The woman of his dreams was getting ready to start a family with him. Cheri was trying to grasp the image of a crying baby and studying and the same time.

Kerry spoiled her after finding out she was pregnant. More than he had before. He took over certain duties in the house like going to the food market. He made sure the laundry was folded when he could remember. He tried to make things comfortable for Cheri.

Cheri noticed and she appreciated it. She tried to be conscious of his gestures and watch her moods. Sometimes it seemed like the hormones won still. As she began to get excited about being a new mommy, she also became nervous about telling her family.

She knew that Thanksgiving was approaching. That meant she would be going to Texas soon. She even thought about waiting to tell them. She was still small and only she and Kerry could tell she was pregnant.

She was also indifferent about possibly seeing Edwin. After she found out she was pregnant, she decided to just move on without an explanation. After all, that is what he did. She had to hear about his baby on the way through her sister. She did not take into account she had been ignoring all of his calls.

It seemed like time past rapidly as the couple waited for their new baby to grow. At her appointment just before Thanksgiving break, the doctor told them they would be able to reveal the gender at their next appointment. That made things even more real for Cheri. She began planning room decor in her head for both genders.

As she packed for her Thanksgiving trip home. She and Kerry discussed revealing the news to her family. He had not told his family yet. Cheri had requested he wait until they were in a safe stage.

"Are you going to tell your mom about the baby?" He asked while she zipped her suitcase.

"I don't think so." She said without looking up.

Kerry paused before he asked his next question, "Does your family know about me?" He was afraid of the answer. His fears were justified.

He had never met her family in three years. She always flew home and flew back. He said hello to her mother over the phone on scant occasions. Even on those few occasions, Cheri never formally introduced him as someone she was in a relationship with. It made him skeptical.

"Yes. My mom asked who you were when I sent them the townhouse lease. They wanted to know if I had a girlfriend named Kerry I was hiding. They even took the understanding approach. My dad could care less. My mom was happy to find out I was moving in with a man." Cheri said smiling.

She continued, "I am worried about telling them I am pregnant, and we are not married."

"Will you assure them I plan on marrying you?" He asked confidently.

"That is not something I know to be a fact. It has only been implied my dear." Cheri refuted with her law lingo.

"You know how I feel about you woman. Now hurry up and pack so I can get you off to the airport." He said smiling.

Chapter 4:
Texas Hold 'Em

Getting through Thanksgiving break was easier than Cheri anticipated. She was not so far along she bore the physical appearance of a pregnant lady. She slept or studied most of the time while she was home. Those behaviors were not out of the ordinary during a school break.

When she was awake and not studying, she ate like a champion fighter. Lucky for her, all four of her sisters and nieces were home. Each time she ate there was a new person in the kitchen. If had been just her and her mom, her mom would have become suspicious.

The day she had been waiting for had finally arrived. On Thanksgiving morning, she woke to the aroma of dinner already in process. Her mom and sisters were in the kitchen as usual. She was the only one that slept in late. Which was unusual.

"Tired darling?" Her mom said as she entered the kitchen. "I swear you have been asleep this whole break."

"Oh mom, it is my last year. It is kicking my tail. But it is almost over thank God." Cheri tried to deflect further reasons for her fatigue.

"Well I am proud of you. You are my baby. Sleep all you want." Her oldest sister Gina chimed in.

"So, how is your boyfriend. Kerry, right?" Julia added. "I have been in New York for almost a year and I have not met him. You guys don't feel bad."

Her mom joined in again, "Why the secrecy baby? What is wrong with him?"

"Wow, were you guys having a who talk about me before I woke up?" Cheri was able to get in.

"Yes." They all said in unison.

"Seriously though," Melissa poked, "What is up? Why haven't we met a guy you live with?"

The floor was open to Cheri. "You guys will meet him really soon I promise. I just wanted to make sure we were serious before I brought him around the family."

That answer seemed to suffice. They turned the conversation to the awkward life circumstances of the rest of the sisters. Cheri was glad even though she might be forced to give up her secret. She and Kerry were getting ready for a baby.

She did her best to help out with the Thanksgiving meal preparation. She laughed, cooked, and enjoyed her family as much as she could. She did not want to sleep the whole time away. However, the baby she was carrying commanded she get some sleep against her will.

After her mom put the stuffing in the oven, she gave in to her unannounced condition.

She also knew a good nap would make up for the time the food had to cook unattended. Collard greens, ham, and other Thanksgiving delicacies slow cooked for hours. She enjoyed the thought of waking up to dinner.

"Mom."

"Yes baby?" Her mother stopped flattening pie crust to give her daughter her attention.

"I am going to take a nap before dinner. You need me to help with anymore prep?" Cheri asked yawning.

"No go rest." Her mom said touching her stomach.

Cheri flinched. Her mom smiled almost instantly. They both knew they knew at that moment. Her mom took her not telling as a hint. She agreed to keep it to herself. But she was excited.

"Is it Kerry's?" Her mom asked. At this point they were whispering.

"Yes." Cheri replied shyly. She was relieved her mom did not seem upset or disappointed.

"I will wake you of you are not up when it is time to eat baby." Her mom said breaking their moment they had to enjoy in silence.

"Thanks, I love you mom!" Cheri exclaimed hugging her mother.

"I love you too."

Cheri retired to a bedroom she shared with her sister Julia when they were home. Her sister Gina lived in Texas with her mom and dad. Julia and Cheri were in New York for their studies. Their baby sister Melissa wanted to move New York with them. She had one more year of high school.

Before she went to sleep, she checked her phone. She had a few messages from Kerry, so she decided to return them before going back to sleep. Lucky for her, he was busy with his family. He had to hurry her off the phone to interact with his own kin that he barely saw.

She woke up from her nap to her mom gently shaking her to wake up. It was a bittersweet moment. The nap was everything she wanted it to be. She was also very ready to eat Thanksgiving dinner with her family.

When she arrived to the dining room, she could see she was last to arrive. Everyone was so busy talking or fixing a plate, no one called her out for sleeping again. She dove right in with her family. She piled her plate up with all the good things her family had prepared.

There were usually too many people to eat at the table if you were late. Family from the region stopped by their house on Thanksgiving Day. It was tradition to visit aunts and uncles houses in the family. Cheri just sat out on the ride to nap instead.

Her mom kept a den free for her children and their children. She made sure they had a comfortable place to eat regardless of the house capacity. She took care of her babies. Cheri ate and caught up with different family members for a few hours.

After a while fatigue caught up with her and she was ready for bed. Besides, she could wake up and eat again while everyone was sleeping. It was a fail proof plan. As she moved toward the kitchen to dispose of a plate, her nephew ran to her and told her someone was outside for her.

"Give me one second." She said.

As she made her way to the door, she saw the luxury SUV sitting in her driveway. She knew who it belonged to instantly. She had been picked up in it the night John Paul had attacked her. Her full stomach suddenly felt empty and sick.

She thought about sending someone to tell Edwin she was sleep. Sadly, she had already sent her nephew with a message from her. Something else hit her as she walked toward the front porch.

She had been with Edwin after her last known period.

She almost vomited as she stepped into the front porch. Her uncles and dad were playing Texas Hold'em and smoking cigarettes. The smell made her run way. It also made her dash off of the porch. This meant she was almost running to meet Edwin.

"Funny you are running to me, but you have been ignoring me for almost 4 months now." Edwin was not happy. His tone was very assertive.

"I was not running to you I was-" she cut herself off. "What are you doing here?" She changed the subject.

"Hmmm. Do we not always see each other on your school break? The only difference is you ignored me the whole time you were away this time. What changed?" He was careful to speak low. He was aware the men sitting on the porch were ready to defend the slightest offense.

"Ed. Edwin, I cannot see you anymore." She said it despite not wanting to. Her stomach fluttered as she spoke with him. It made her sick along with the cigarette aroma outside.

"Why?" He was irritated, but he held his composure.

"Why does it matter? You are married. You have a baby coming right?" Cheri was becoming upset herself.

"Can we go somewhere and talk?" Edwin wanted some privacy.

"No go home to your wife and baby!" Cheri was angry at this point. She was careful not to scream. She knew her dad would be listening as best as he could.

"When are you flying out? Let me take you to the airport." Edwin offered.

"No." Cheri turned and walked away back towards the house.

If the porch were not full of men, he would have grabbed her to come back. By this time, her mom had come out to see what man came to see Cheri. Her mom asked her who Edwin was, but she just replied, "Nobody."

Edwin and Cheri dated when Cheri was not allowed to have a boyfriend. She hid him from her family for years. He had actually been in the very house her parents still lived in many times. They just broke up before she was allowed to publicly date.

He decided it was in his best interest to leave. He wanted to storm in the house after Cheri.

He just did not want to take the chance of having to explain why he was arrested chasing another woman to his wife. He was not done trying to talk to Cheri though.

Cheri went to take the nap she had planned to take before Edwin showed up. She was upset after seeing him for a few reasons. She figured the nap would be best to help her relax. She wished she would have stayed in New York.

She told him she was done with him. She knew deep down that was far from the truth. Seeing him upset her so much she had to admit she was still in love with him. She also had to admit he might have fathered the baby she was carrying. That thought alone made her want to get to New York as soon as possible.

She vowed to stay in New York until the baby was born. She would just ignore Edwin from there. It had worked the first four months of her pregnancy. She would make it work for five more months.

She also considered changing her phone number so that he would have less access. She just did not want anything to seem suspicious to Kerry. She also did not want Edwin to ruin the family legacy they were starting.

She figured he had his own wife and family. That meant she had the right to have her own. They would have to move own regardless of their history. She loved Kerry and the way he loved her. Edwin's new burdens were not worth hurting Kerry.

She was thankful that Thanksgiving was on Thursday. She had to fly back to New York for class on Monday. Her sister and mom took her to the airport on Friday night. Her mom was in tears as she entered the terminal. She wanted to tell her sister, but she also wanted to respect Kerry's feelings. Her mom just knew as a mom.

She boarded her plane grateful Edwin had not tried to contact her since leaving the house. She took it as a sign he might have listened to her. She was ready to see Kerry. Her mom took great care of her. She was still ready to get back to the care of Kerry.

She was disappointed when she landed at the airport. Rubi was waiting to pick her up instead of Kerry. Kerry had specifically said he was coming. She was inquisitive.

"Hey girl! I am grateful for the ride, but where is Kerry. Is he ok?" Cheri asked Rubi concerned.

"He is fine girl relax. He got tied up and asked me to pick you up." Rubi tried to ease her concern.

"Tied up doing what?" Cheri wanted more.

"Ugh. I cannot tell you. That is it." Rubi became short.

"Really? You are my best friend!" Cheri was confused.

"Exactly. That should tell you I will not do anything detrimental to you. I have just been sworn to secrecy." Rubi was obviously excited about something. Cheri decided to play along.

The two chatted the rest of the way about the holiday. Rubi still did not know Cheri was pregnant, so Cheri only talked about family. She was becoming anxious as they arrived at the house. She had text Kerry, but he had not responded.

When she pulled up, the house was unusually dark. She gave Rubi her keys and asked her to open the house while she grabbed her bags. As she walked into the doorway with her first bag, the lights popped on and a host of friends and Kerry's family was in their townhome.

Kerry was in the opening on one knee asking her to marry him. She felt overwhelmed. She had just left a man that could possibly be the dad to the baby she was carrying. She had another host of preconceived notions. She realized the crowd was waiting for an answer. She finally said "Yes."

Chapter 5: Gender Reveal

Cheri made Kerry promise not to set a wedding date until she had delivered the baby. She did not want to add wedding planning to the stress of school and a baby. He agreed that would be best. He just wanted to make sure she understood he intended to make her his wife.

He did a good job with the ring too. She was happy with his selection. Cheri was even more happy about the proposal. She could tell that Kerry had put much thought into their engagement night.

There was only one component missing. Her family. Being around her sisters made her realize much time had passed them by. Julia was beyond accurate. She lived right in the city; it was time she met Kerry.

She could help Cheri figure out how to explain a fiancé and new baby to the family. Time was passing. Cheri was beginning to show physical signs of pregnancy. She also felt lonely with all the extra work Kerry had picked up.

Kerry had already told his mom about the baby. She also had the pleasure of attending their surprise engagement. It was time for her to tell her family. She just hoped everyone else was as open as her mom. Her sisters were not too fond of the guys she dated in the past.

"Hey love, I have a question." Cheri said as they sat for an early December breakfast.

"What is it sweetie?" Kerry asked never looking up from his morning news tab.

"You know I have a sister here in New York, right? I was wondering if she could go to the appointment with me on Monday?" Cheri asked nervously.

Kerry put his tablet down and sat up. "Why? We will be finding out the gender?" He asked.

"Your family already knows everything. I want to tell my family in a special way too." She continued.

Kerry was not in agreement. "We can go down and tell them everything on Christmas. I'll just book a flight to go with you." He suggested.

Cheri's stomach began to feel sick. She decided to stay away from Texas until she delivered the baby. A blind man could tell she was pregnant. There was one man she did not want to know at all.

"Kerry, do this for me. I have been doing this your way the whole time. I am asking for one exception to your rules concerning my child." She said a bit firmly.

He sat back in his chair without responding. Then he said, "Alright, take your sister. But I get to meet your family at Christmas still. I have no clue what I am marrying into. To be flat out honest, I want to know." He said back firmly.

He also had a point. Between after eating fatigue and thinking about finals, she could not think of an excuse fast enough. Not one that would suffice him not meeting his child's grandparents. She just agreed. She would try to stay in the house.

She was excited that Kerry was allowing Julia to go to her appointment. She hoped that she was free. She was completing her undergraduate degree while starting a career in real estate. The two sisters had schedules that did not allow them to see each other. It was easy for Cheri to hide her pregnancy.

She rushed to her phone to call Julia after breakfast. "Baby Ju. What are you doing?" She asked even more excited she had picked up on a Saturday morning.

"In a meeting are you ok?" Julia asked hurriedly.

"Ugh yes. Make sure to call me back!" Cheri said quickly.

"I will love you." Julia hung up the phone without waiting for a response.

She did call back. She also agreed to meet Cheri on that following Monday. Cheri did not tell her why they were meeting. She just told her what time to be ready to be picked up.

The morning of, Kerry was not a very inviting person. Cheri took it as he was a little sour about not going to the appointment. She left him to get over it. She was too excited about seeing her sister.

"Oh my God." Julia said as she sat in the car looking at her sister. "You know, Gina said you were pregnant, but I told her, I live in New York. I would know. But I don't know apparently." She continued.

"Look you still have to keep it a secret. We are just going to see the gender today." Cheri calmed her down.

"What?" Julia grabbed both ears in excitement. "Is it the Kerry guys baby? Wait did he leave you or something? Does he know you are pregnant?"

"Pipe down Dan Rather. He is at home pouting now that I am taking you!" Cheri said excited.

Julia continued her questions until they arrived at the appointment. Once there, they found out that Cheri was having a baby girl together. They both cried for a little while before Cheri was able to drive them home. They were crying for different reasons.

Julia was crying because her favorite sister was having a baby. She was excited and honored she allowed her to share that moment with her. It also made her realize how much time had passed. She felt guilty for not spending more time with family.

Cheri was crying about her secret. She felt that the baby girl belonged to Edwin. Before the appointment she looked at a calendar to get a better idea of whose baby it was. The dates that her doctors confirmed matched the night she spent with Edwin.

Edwin had not stop calling her since she returned to New York. Now that Kerry wanted to go to Texas for Christmas, she would have to figure out how to talk to him. She feared if she did not, he would pop up at the house again. The problem was Kerry would be there this time.

As she dropped her sister off, they vowed to see each other more. Julia inquired about meeting Kerry. Cheri assured her it would be soon. Julia hurried her off to tell Kerry the great news. Cheri felt like she should have been calling Edwin.

There were only a couple of weeks left until Christmas. She challenged herself to make the call before she boarded her flight. She wanted to focus on her new fiancé first. She knew he would be excited. She wanted to be excited for him.

When she arrived he was waiting by the door. If it were not so cold, he would have been waiting on the street curb. He purposely did not call her while she was gone. He wanted to respect the time with her sister.

"So?" He said before she could take off her coat.

"It is a girl!" She said smiling.

Kerry rushed to pick her up off her feet. He had a little trouble due to her extra weight gain. They both laughed knowing he used to pick her up with ease. He settled for extra kisses and hugs.

"Can I name her?" He asked Cheri.

"Sure." She said hesitantly.

"What? You do not trust me?" He asked jokingly.

"No, I do not. I am wondering what I am agreeing to." She replied smiling.

"Awww. Come on. You will get final approval." Kerry reassured her.

"Ok that makes me feel better. Can we grab lunch? Little baby is hungry." She added.

The two had lunch and the rest of their day together. Kerry had taken off to find out the gender. Cheri had one more final before they flew to Texas. Going to Texas made her nervous.

She was even more nervous to talk to Edwin. She wondered if he would listen when she asked him to stay away. They had no regard for each other's boundaries. They never had. She hoped he would listen, just for a few days.

The days that led up to their flight seemed to fly by fast. Cheri and Kerry had been invited to a Christmas party that they decided to attend. Their mutual friends, Jamie and Max, had a condo in the downtown area where they entertained guest. While Cheri dressed for the party, she thought it would be a good time for Kerry to be distracted. This meant she would possibly have a diversion to call Edwin.

"You almost ready to go baby?" Kerry asked, breaking her train of thought.

"Yes, I was just putting on make-up. Then I will finish with my dress. I feel like a whale!" She replied picturing herself in her dress.

"Baby you will be the most beautiful whale in the sea!" Kerry said laughing.

"Not the right answer Ker. Lie to me for the rest of my pregnancy please?" Cheri shot back at him.

"I know at least you are ready for the good food tonight?" Kerry said trying to redeem himself.

"Why? So I can be an even bigger beautiful whale?" Cheri would not let him off the hook that easy.

"No baby, you know I did not mean any harm." Kerry was waving his white flag.

"I am actually ready to see Jamie. We have not been able to hang out since I have been so pregnant. Our nights of wine are not as interesting without a wine glass in my hand too." She did not want to draw any more blood.

"Well you only have a few more months babe. You will have your beloved wine glass soon." Kerry added.

Cheri actually wished he would leave her to finish getting dressed. She had made her mind up to call Edwin. It seemed like her stomach, nor the baby, would stop moving since she mentally committed. The feeling was so strong, she attributed it to more than just nerves.

She was not nervous about calling him. She actually looked forward to talking to him. A piece of her missed him. She was nervous about his answer to her request.

74

He would either respect her feelings and agreed. Or, he would completely ignore her request and show up when he pleased. This is something he had always done. This will be the first time she cannot keep Kerry out of Texas, however.

As soon as they arrived to the party, she made her split from Kerry. They were regular guest in the Jamie and Max's home. She said hello to whoever was on her way to Jamie's spare bedroom. She kept the greetings short on purpose. The faster she dialed Edwin, the sooner she would be able to relax.

Once she reached the room, she checked to make sure her privacy was secure. She reached into her clutch purse and retrieved her cell phone. Her fingers trembled as she dialed. He had tried to call her dozens of times since she had returned to New York. This is the first call she had returned.

"Hello-"

"Ed I-" Cheri started as soon as she heard his voice. She had her apology ready.

"- You have reached the voicemail box Edwin Frank." Edwin's mailbox cut her off as he completed his recorded voice mailbox greeting.

Cheri threw her phone in her clutch in frustration. She mumbled "how dare he ignore my call?" Thinking no one heard her.

"Who girl?"

Cheri spun around to see Jamie standing in the doorway. She had not heard the door open thinking about Edwin. She was also not prepared to answer the question. Jamie was a mutual friend of hers and Kerry. The only man she knew of in Cheri's life was Kerry.

"Nobody." She answered quickly.

Jamie gave her a suspicious look before she said, "Well I just saw Kerry and I then came looking for you. How are You? How is being pregnant in a New York winter?"

"The winter is not the concern. It is my wine prohibition versus law school finals that has me stressed." Cheri said glad Jamie did not ask more questions about the phone call.

"You are almost done with school and pregnancy. In a matter of months, it will all be worth it." Said Jamie to encourage her friend.

"I know, I know. Well do you guys have any good food?" Cheri really was hungry. She just wanted to get the call to Edwin over with.

"Of course, follow me." Jamie headed towards the kitchen.

The party was wonderful. The ambience was nice, and the guest were socialites of the area. Cheri simply had a hard time enjoying herself. She was distracted by her failed call to Edwin. Kerry could tell she was distracted by something too. He just did not know what.

Chapter 6:
The Wrong
Dates Match

Cheri tried calling Edwin a few more times before she flew to Texas. Her attempts were all ignored. Part of her wanted to know why he was ignoring her. The other part hoped that he would continue to ignore her until she returned to New York.

She was also nervous about Kerry meeting her family for the first time. She knew they would approve of him. She was still just as nervous as if they would not. Plus, she also had to reveal to the rest of her family she was pregnant.

Her dad met them at the airport to drive them home. The rest of the family was at the house waiting for them to arrive. Everyone new Cheri was in a serious relationship. No one had ever laid eyes on the fellow before.

Her dad had a small suspicion, but he kept his concern to himself. Once he laid eyes on Kerry, he remembered the guy that showed up to his house for Thanksgiving. He also remembered the young man's actions. His actions gave off a tone that he loved Cheri. He also thought it was strange Cheri gave him the same tone back.

Her mom was starting to speculate if it was really a guy at one point. She wondered if Cheri had made him up so she did not seem lonely. She came up with many theories since Cheri seemed to hide him. She was excited to meet him. Especially since he was a the father of her new grandchild.

When they arrived to the house. It seemed like the whole family was waiting outside. Mom, sisters, nieces, nephews, aunt's, and a few cousins lined the front porch and entry. Cheri's stomach and the baby were turning flips by that point.

I small piece of her made her scan the yard and road for Edwin. With that many people at her house, it would not be strange if he heard she was home. Kerry noticed his fiancée looked concerned. He thought that was strange since they were going to her home.

"Hey you. You okay?" Kerry asked Cheri concerned.

"Yes of course. Just ready to get out." Cheri said as her dad pulled into his driveway.

Her mom immediately ran to the car as her dad parked. "Hey baby!" Her mom said half hugging her and half pulling her from the car.

"Hey mom." She said trying to catch her breath. Her mom storming her took her aback a bit.

"Hey baby. I did not tell them." Her mom said whispering in her ear.

"Tell them wh-" Cheri could not finish her statement before her other sisters ran to the car too.

"So? Got anything to tell us?" Gina asked smiling.

"Yeah?" Melissa chimed in right after her.

"It seems like you already know what you want to hear." Cheri said teasing them.

"They do, but they want it to come from you." Julia added.

"Judas." Cheri said smirking at Julia.

"I slipped out in a drunk dial too sis." Julia said laughing.

"Well guys, I am pregnant." Cheri said finally making her way out of the car.

"Hi I am Kerry." Kerry said interrupting their moment.

The sisters did not like the emotional interruption, but Cheri's mom did not mind. "Hi honey, I am Diedra." Cheri's mom said extending her hand. "Let me show you into the house while these ladies catch up. It could be a while."

Cheri noticed her mom swept Kerry a way. She was too caught up with her sisters to stop them. She had no worries with them meeting him. She only worried Edwin would show up.

It was the day before Christmas eve. They would fly back to New York the day after Christmas. Cheri hoped Edwin kept ignoring her for at least the next four days. She had no idea how she would explain Edwin to Kerry or Kerry to Edwin.

Cheri greeted the rest of her family as they walked into the house. Everyone was excited for her and wanted to touch her belly. She decided to go find Kerry to make sure he was comfortable. She was stopped by her baby sister before she could find him.

"Hey, you remember your friend Ed from high school?" Melissa said innocently.

"Yes, what about him?" Cheri became nervous.

"I heard he just had a baby boy." Melissa said genuinely happy for him.

Cheri stomach and heart fluttered. Her hormones commanded her to cry. Her pride and secret held back the tears. She did not want to seem strange reacting emotionally to another woman's husband.

"Well I hope that baby boy is as successful as his dad. He will have a great role model." Cheri forced herself to say.

"Hey baby I have been looking for you. You okay?" Kerry asked walking up behind Cheri.

"Yes. Melissa do you mind if I take Kerry upstairs? I still need to decompress from the trip myself." Cheri asked her baby sister.

"No go right ahead. I will see you two later." Melissa said and then disappeared to the den.

"So, you want a tour?" Cheri said turning to Kerry.

"Sure." He replied with a smile. "You know, I was wondering what you were hiding. Your folks seem alright so far."

Cheri smiled and started showing him the house without a reply. She normally had a witty rebuttal for her fiancé. Instead, she kept replaying the news her sister gave her in her head. She wondered if that was why Edwin had been ignoring her.

The next day, Kerry and Cheri planned to see her hometown. They would not be able to see much. Many businesses and institutions were closed for Christmas Eve. Still, Kerry was interested in where his lady was from. They decided to go out anyway.

"Mom, can I borrow your car? Dad is going fishing soon." Cheri and Kerry needed a way around. They had flown to Texas, so their vehicles were in New York.

"Sure, but I need to run to the store. I am out of vanilla extract and foil. Will you come with me?" Her mom asked whole heartedly. She saw a chance to spend some time with her pregnant child without the other daughters noticing.

"Seriously mom?" Cheri would rather eat or nap than walk through a store on Christmas eve.

"Please honey?" Her mom fluttered her eyelashes.

"Ugh ok, let me tell Kerry I will be right back." Cheri said reluctantly.

Her mom was just as happy as could be. It was not all about Cheri. She knew the stores would be packed because of the holidays. Cheri would make for good company as she shopped and waited in lines.

When they arrived at the store, it was as packed as they thought it would be. All the meal preppers were gathering their last-minute items. The aisle was full, and so were the checkout lines. Cheri wanted to get out as fast as they could. She could tell her feet would be swollen by the time they were done gathering just a couple of items.

"Mom let's divide and conquer." Cheri suggested. "You go grab the extract and I will get the foil. Meet me back at checkout counter number nine. What do you say?"

"Good idea honey." Diedra said agreeing.

Cheri took off toward where she thought the foil could would be. It was not a store she was familiar with, she eventually had to ask for help. After a few extra minutes of dialogue and help, she had foil. She turned to meet her mom at checkout number nine.

As she approached the checkout counter, she was glad to see her mom already in line. That meant the wait would be less. The closer she got to her mom she realized her mom was talking with someone. The closer she got, she realized that someone was Edwin.

Cheri panicked. She was stuck between ditching her mother or facing Edwin. She was growing so fatigued from the trip, she decided to face him. At least she could tell him not come by her parents' house.

"Here she is now." Her mom said as Cheri approached. "I remembered this young man stopped by the house. I told him you were in town again with your fiancé."

As Diedra finished her words Edwin spun around to face Cheri. He went to hug her, but he stopped as he noticed her growing stomach. After a short pause, he hugged her anyway. Cheri stood like a statue as he embraced her. The whole while the baby in her stomach seemed to be doing flips.

"Long time not talk." Edwin said releasing his hug. "I see you have been busy."

Cheri just smiled, she felt awkward.

"How far along are you?" Edwin asked breaking the awkward silence.

"She is five going on six months." Cheri's mom answered for her in excitement.

"Really." Is all Edwin could manage to say.

Before the conversation could reveal more, the cashier attracted Cheri and her mom's attention to checkout and go. Cheri even forgot to tell him to stay away from her parent's house. She was so shocked to had run into him. She was speechless because she felt he knew just by the look in his eyes.

Edwin could only think about Cheri as he drove home. He tried to count back to the day he had picked her up after John Paul's attack. He was no expert on pregnancy timing, but he was an educated man. He was positive Cheri conceived around the time they were together.

He all of a sudden, he felt disgusted with himself for ignoring her phone calls. He thought he was justified when he did it. She seemed to have made it clear she wanted to move on. She had ignored him for so long, he decided to focus on his wife and growing family.

Edwin's first instinct was to meet Cheri at her parent's house. He was also on his way home. He knew his wife and new baby boy were home waiting for him to return. He figured he would go take care of them first.

When he arrived home, he gave his wife the baby items she had sent him the store for. He held his baby boy and played with him until he cried for a feeding. Once they had gotten the baby off to a nap, Edwin thought it would be a good time to sneak away. Maybe his wife could even catch snooze or two.

"Where are you getting ready to go?" His wife asked when she noticed him grooming himself.

"Just out for a little bit. Get some air and think. I will be right back." He said calmly.

"Exactly where to get some air?" She asked.

"I really haven't decided. I am just getting ready. Maybe walk the block. Maybe swing by the gym." He was trying his best to seem transparent.

"I want to get out too. Maybe we can take the stroller and go together?" She suggested.

"Na part of this is for some alone time. You can go when I get back though. I do not like taking my son out unnecessarily." He said still calm.

"Is she in town?" She said coming into the bathroom where he was.

"What? Who?" Edwin replied. He knew exactly who "she" was.

"Cheri. Is Cheri in town?" His wife knew he knew too.

Edwin felt his blood pressure rise. He still decided to keep things cool. "I do not know. That is not my concern."

"I am not stupid Edwin!" His wife was losing her composure.

"I never said you were." He said quietly grabbing her hand.

She yanked it away. "You go out for hours and do not even have enough respect to answer the phone. Do you think you would show up to a full house of people, argue with another women, and I would not find out?"

He felt bad. He knew she was exactly right. This was not the first time they had discussed his high school sweetheart. This was not their first talk about his behavior when Cheri was in town.

Despite his wife feelings, he had to see Cheri. He had to get an answer about his assumptions. He decided to just go. He would deal with his wife once he returned.

"I am not done talking!" She said as he walked away from her.

"I am." He said nonchalantly.

He went to grab his shoes, and she snatched them from his hand. "You are not going to see her."

"Just stop. I am not going to see anybody." He tried to maintain his poise.

"You are not going anywhere." She held his shoes and positioned herself in front of their front door.

"Look I am sorry about how you feel. I am going." He said as he tried to brush past her.

She instantly grabbed the collar of his shirt while his back was to her. She started to land punches on him as he whirled around to face her. Her anger intensified as he tried to grab control of her arms. He did not want to be blamed for domestic violence. He did his best to protect himself without lashing back.

He wrestled with her until she had tired out. She still attempted to cling to him despite her fatigue. He was shocked at her behavior. But he understand her plight. He just had to talk to Cheri because in his head, the wrong dates matched.

Chapter 7: A Whole Man is Looking

Lucky for Cheri, she made it back to New York without Edwin popping up at her parents' house. She was actually excited about how the trip went. Her family welcomed Kerry with open arms. She felt good about not hiding him and her pregnancy anymore.

Kerry was also happy about their trip. It was much more than he had expected. He felt Cheri hid so much of her life from him. After meeting everyone, he wondered why? She belonged to a wonderful family.

The trip motivated him to solidify the bond of his own family. " Hey baby?"

"Yes?" Cheri said eating a bowl of cereal on morning.

"What if we go ahead and get married. Nothing fancy. We can go to the court house." Kerry suggested.

"No way. This is my last semester. I need to pass the bar. I need to somehow pass a baby through my vagina. I am not interested in the courthouse picture. Pass." She said bluntly.

"But we can still do all those things later. We would just get married now." Kerry insisted.

"We already agreed to wait." Cheri said dismissively. "I am stressed enough."

When he heard the word stress, Kerry decided to concede for the time being. He was still anxious to marry his fiancé. He just wished she was on the same page as him. She seemed kind of distant while she was in Texas. Her vibe had not changed much once the returned home.

Instead of accusing or questioning her he blamed her hormones. He hoped things would return to normal between them once the baby was born. He was very excited about having his first baby girl. He was also nervous about being a dad. The pregnancy was unexpected for the two of them.

After her cereal, Cheri retreated to her bedroom. She was due in a few months. She felt like she had to either sleep or eat constantly. Failing to do either was a disaster for whom ever was around her.

As she entered the bedroom, she heard her phone vibrating. When she saw it was Edwin, she decided to ignore him. She had made it back to New York without Kerry discovering him. She felt she was in the clear.

After he discovered she had left, Edwin turned to his brother Nathan. He knew that he could only trust a few people with such a delicate secret. He did not want to make a scene, and there was a chance it was not his child. He and his wife had a big enough rift between then.

"Nate, what are you doing?" Edwin asked his younger brother.

"Nothing, nothing at all. What do you need my brother?" He said kindly.

"I need to talk to you." Edwin went on.

"I am listening." Nathan replied.

"Look. Cheri is pregnant." Edwin said and paused.

"So?" His brother was not aware of his infidelity.

"I think the baby is mine." Edwin paused for his brother's reaction.

"Hmm. Why you think that? You married bruh. What you been out here doing? That is your New York chick right?" His brother asked non-judgmental.

"Yes. It was one night. But something is off. She left town before I could speak with her. I am thinking about flying to NY." Edwin added.

"You should slow down. What will you tell your wife?" Nathan wondered.

"That you and I have a guys trip for a few days. I know where she goes to school. I want to surprise her." Edwin sounded hopeful about his plan.

"You mean to tell me; you want to fly across the country? You want to see a woman who you might find? You want to talk to her about a baby that might be yours?" Nathan asked incredulously.

"I know what it sounds like. But I need to do this brother." Edwin refuted.

"Aghhhh. I am with you. I just hope, this does not blow up in your face. You have a beautiful family. I want to look into a business venture out that way. Funny you called me with this." Nathan added.

"Ok. I will make plans and forward them to you." Edwin said excited.

"I think you are a fool, but ok." Nathan said before hanging up.

For the next few weeks leading up to his trip, Edwin tried to contact Cheri. He never was able to reach her. He was still determined to see her. He wanted answers about the baby she was carrying.

He was able to convince his wife he was going to help Nathan. He did not feel good about lying to her. He also did not feel good about possibly having another child across the country. He wanted to put his suspicion to rest. Seeing Cheri was a bonus.

Once they arrived in New York, he commenced his plan to find her. He tried for a couple of days to find her on her campus. He looked for her in law libraries in the city. He even tried to locate her sister that was in the city. He hoped at least one trail would lead him to Cheri.

While out his brother had an interesting find. Nathan missed the deal he originally had interest in. However, he was able to find a foreclosing restaurant while they strolled the streets. While his brother looked for his missing pregnant woman, he meet with brokers and owners.

When it was time to fly back to Texas, Edwin flew back empty handed. Nathan flew back with a successful deal in his pocket. The whole trip was not in vain. Edwin took his failed attempt as a sign he should move on again.

Cheri was oblivious that a whole man had been canvassing the city for her. She and Kerry were caught in a whirlwind of good news and baby anxiety. They were prepping for the baby girl that was soon to arrive. Cheri was also having pregnancy complications.

The doctors mandated that she spend her last few weeks off of her feet. Since they did not want to risk the baby's health, her professors sent tutors and lectured to help her stay abreast in school. Kerry was a constant help while he was home.

"Hey baby!" Kerry says one day bursting through the door.

"What are you excited about handsome?" Cheri asked.

"Guess who landed the job?" He asked playfully.

Cheri jumped to her feet forgetting the doctors' orders. "Congratulations!"

"Thank you honey!" He replied. "Now off of your feet please."

"Sure, but that makes me wonder." She added.

"Wonder what baby?" He asked concerned.

"As an intern you spent a lot of time away. What will I do when the baby comes? Especially now you made it as an associate." Cheri wanted to know.

"Maybe we can get you a Nanny? I have to money now." Kerry suggested.

"No stranger will be in my house with my baby. I will be vulnerable." Cheri refuted.

"Well what do you want to do?" Kerry wondered.

"I want to go home. To my mom's." Cheri said matter of factly.

"Absolutely not." Kerry chided. You will not take my newborn across the country. My mom can help up out."

"I do not want that. I do not think it is fair you do this. We did not know you would get the job." Cheri tried to convince him.

"We knew it was a possibility. I do not think you leaving is the solution." Kerry was becoming irritated. "It sounds like you already had this planned."

"I am scared. I want my momma. It is that simple. We will not be gone long. Maybe just the summer while I get a hang of being a mom." Cheri said in rebuttal.

"No." Kerry became short with her.

"I am going." Cheri was never good at being backed into a corner.

"You can go. My child will stay here, with me." Kerry said and walked away.

If Cheri was not on bed rest, she would have taken a flight to Texas to prove a point. She and Kerry fought more often the closer she came to giving birth. She decided to book a ticket for herself and the baby after her due date despite Kerry's feelings. She would try to convince him until it was time to go.

The baby was due a month before finals. Her professors assured her she would be graduating as long as she completed her current assignments. She felt it was unrealistic for Kerry to expect her to be alone or with his mother. She wanted to be comfortable with her own mother.

Chapter 8:
DNA

Baby Edith was born on time as expected.
She was one of the most beautiful babies many

people had ever seen. Kerry was in love with her at first site. He was so anxious to meet his first child.

Cheri was also excited. She could finally have a glass or two of wine. Nine months of pregnancy and law school was not a piece of cake. She was also ready to meet her little bundle of joy. Her mom and dad had flown down to see the birth. She had planned to fly back with them. She just did not know how to tell Kerry.

Watching him interact with Edith for the first time gave her chills. She felt bad for separating the two of them. She also did not want to spend the summer alone with a newborn. It scared her.

Her parents stayed until she and the baby were released from the hospital. Once they returned home, Cheri felt the pressure to tell Kerry. She knew soon her parents would inquire about leaving.

"Kerry." She said as Kerry cuddled Edith.

"Yes mama? Get over here with us." Kerry was grinning from ear to ear.

"You have to go back to work in a few days." Cheri started.

"Yes, I know. What is wrong are you ok?" Kerry asked.

"Well I expressed my interest in us going to Texas before she was born." Cheri added, but Kerry interrupted.

"I know, and I apologize for my reaction. If your parents could travel with you, I would feel better about it." He answered.

She was relieved. "Do you mind us going in a few days? We have a few appointments here before I go."

"I would rather not at all. But I understand. Look at this baby. Imagine if I was trying to take her from you?" Kerry was sad and Cheri could tell.

"I would be devastated." Cheri admitted.

"I am worse off than that just thinking about her going. What about school?" Kerry asked.

"I was allowed to take my finals early. I am just awaiting grades to post. I will forfeit walking the stage." She said sadly.

"Well I will enjoy you guys while you are here." Kerry said to lighten the mood.

The next few days, Kerry really tried to enjoy his family. He hated that Cheri was taking his new baby to Texas. He also had to be realistic about his work schedule. He had to decide between seeing his family or taking care of his family. Taking care of them came first.

Cheri's parents traveling with them put him at ease. He made sure to see them off to the airport. He demanded she let him know that safely landed. He focused on work while they were not around. He made plans to go see them as soon as they landed.

Cheri was glad to be at home once they arrived. Her mom and dad were very hands on with their help. She was able to study and get ready for her Bar Exam. The extra pairs of hands were much needed to. Edith was a big eater and a light sleeper.

Cheri was blown away by the maintenance a newborn required. She was grateful to have her parents. She was glad about her decision. She could only imagine trying to study alone in New York with a screaming baby.

One day while she was studying, her mom notified her she had a visitor. Many of their family members stopped by the house to see her and the baby. She hoped whoever it was did not stay long. She wanted to finish studying the section she was working on.

"Who is here ma?" Cheri asked looking around the empty living room.

"He is outside. He said he'd wait on the porch." Her mom replied.

She hoped it was not her cousin from down the road. He always wanted to talk about the weather and sports. Cheri needed that precious time to study. She wanted to be ready for her exam by the time she returned to New York. Her thoughts were halted as she stepped out into the porch.

"You look good to just have delivered a baby." Edwin said as she stepped through the door frame.

"Why are you here?" Cheri asked combatively.

"Why am I here Cheri?" Edwin paused. "What did you have? Boy or girl?"

"Edwin, I want you to leave." Cheri said ignoring his questions.

"Why won't you answer me?" Edwin inquired.

"It is not your business. Your wife and your son should be your concern." Cheri snapped at him.

"They are. And so are you. That has never been a problem until now. What has changed babe?" Edwin asked incredulously.

"I obviously have a family now. What we are doing. It has to stop. I have said this before." Cheri said folding her arms.

Edwin stood up from his chair and walked towards Cheri. She was still standing by the front door. "Is that baby mine?" He asked looking at her and refusing to break his stare.

Cheri felt nauseous instantly. "No Edwin leave. Now." Losing their staring contest.

"Cheri look at me." Edwin said grabbing her elbow.

"Let me go and leave. Seriously Edwin. I do not have to tell you a thing about my child." She said freeing herself from his grip.

"But why would you not share unless you had something to hide?" Edwin was getting frustrated.

"The only person that owes you an explanation is the woman you are married to. I am not her, right? I am happy. What we had; it is done. If you happened to be her dad, would you feel comfortable with me letting another man see her behind your back?" Cheri retorted.

"Her?" Edwin stepped back.

"Cheri, she needs a feeding." Cheri's mom said bringing the screaming newborn to the door.

"Mom take her back inside please!" Cheri tried to say quickly.

It was too late. Edwin, Cheri, Deidra, and a hungry Edith were all on the porch. Cheri hurriedly grabbed the crying baby and rushed into the house. One she needed to feed her. Two she was hoping Edwin did not get a good look at her.

Her mom saw Edwin to his vehicle. However, he was far from done with Cheri. He saw all he needed to see. He saw that the little girl on the porch was his baby. She was a lighter version of his son, with beautiful curly hair.

"Hello?" Nathan answered yelling.

"Hey, where are you?" Edwin asked his brother.

"I had to fly back to New York to monitor my restaurant project. I'll be back Saturday. What is going on?" Nathan told him.

"Oh, so you are big timing in New York all of a sudden?" Edwin joked.

"You know I flow with my cash brother." Nathan said in a cool tone.

"Speaking of New York. She is here. I saw the baby. She did not want me to. But by a twist of fate I did." Edwin paused.

"And?" Nathan wanted to know.

"I believe that is my daughter man. She looks just like baby Eli." Edwin continued.

"Wow. So, what do you plan on doing?" Nathan wondered.

"That is the thing. I do not know. She is denying the baby is mine." Edwin said sadly.

"Why are you fighting this man? Do you know how many men wish a baby mama would let them off the hook? I think it is a sign and a chance to fix your marriage." Nathan added.

"She is not just some baby mama. And I will never willingly leave my kids." Edwin said.

"I hear you. It just seems like you are making trouble for yourself." Nathan conceded.

"I understand. I also want to be a part of my child's life." Edwin told him.

"A child that is possibly yours?" Nathan challenged him.

"I need to find that out for sure." Edwin went on. "If she will not answer, I will have her served."

"Like a paternity test?" Nathan sounded lost.

"Yes, exactly like that." Edwin assured him.

Edwin made a few more attempts to reach out to Cheri. All of them were thwarted. He did not feel comfortable to keep showing up at the house. Mostly because of their last interaction. He was convinced Cheri was going to try and get her way. He knew he would have to go around her.

He could not be overly aggressive. He had to be careful of his wife's overbearing prying. He was careful to have an attorney separate from theirs draft his petition. He requested the lawyer only correspond with him during his scheduled office hours.

He planned to secretly launch a family court filing. He wanted to know if the baby girl was his or not. He had a strong suspicious she was his because of Cheri's behavior. He could tell she was hiding the truth.

Cheri feared Edwin would not back down. She decided a screaming baby and law books was better than being home when Edwin returned. She arranged for Kerry to chaperone her and the baby to

New York. He was so excited about their homecoming; he did not ask many questions.

He flew to Texas to pick up his new baby and fiance. He was hoping she would be more open to their getting married too. Things were going well in his new position. He wanted to balance the other part of his life. He wanted to make Cheri his wife.

Thinking she was in Texas still; Edwin had the petition for paternity filed in Texas. He was hoping the process would not take long. He only feared the truth coming out for his family's sake. He also feared another man was raising his child. He felt it was only right he tried to find out.

Deidra called a few weeks after the baby and Cheri called home. "Hey love how is my grandbaby?"

"Good mom, I am making it better than I thought." Cheri said happy to hear from her mom.

"Yea it will all come naturally. The second one will be easier too." Deidra hinted.

"Slow down mom, I a barely getting the hang of the first one." Cheri laughed.

"Hey I called because you have a letter here. It looks important." Her mom got serious.

"Well open it mom. It is not like I can." Cheri pushed her.

"Are you sure? It is from the State's Attorney General." Her mom was hesitant.

"Yes, mom it might be a job offer. Even though I have not applied for job." Cheri joked.

"Ok." Her mom paused to open it. "It says, blah blah blah.. You are being petitioned for the paternity findings of unnamed minor born on 04-26-" she cut her mom off.

"Mom what is the name of the petitioner?" Cheri asked.

"Wait." Her mom searched the document. "Edwin Frank?"

"Mom I need to call you back." Cheri said abruptly.

"Are they talking about Edith? Who is Edwin?" Her mom was inquisitive.

"Mom I can't- just let me call you back!" Cheri said trying to control her emotions.

"Well ok. I hope everything is alright." Her mom said sensing her frustration.

"It will be." She assured her mother.

Cheri immediately called Edwin after she and her mom were off the phone. She could not believe the nerve he had to petition her for custody. She did not envision he would go that far. Since he did, she had to neutralize the situation.

She did not want to explain to her fiancé that another man was fighting for paternity of their baby. Even if that man had a vested stake. She and Edwin made the mistake of sleeping together. She was sure it would not happen again. She just had to keep him away from her child.

Chapter 9:
Summoned

Cheri was an aspiring officer of the court.
She also had her own court date to appear in. She

knew she could not ignore the summon. It would impact her unstarted career negatively.

She made attempts to reconcile with Edwin during the months leading up to the set court date. He refused to do anything other than see Edith. She considered letting him visit to appease him. She just did not want to risk Kerry or someone else catching her in New York with another man.

"Please, drop this. You are barking up the wrong tree." Cheri pleaded with Edwin one late night.

"You can send her DNA right now and I could handle this privately." He replied.

"Listen to yourself. You are obsessed. Drop this petition Ed." She continued.

"Do you love me?" Edwin cut her off.

"You are sick. I am engaged and you are married. Why are you doing this? To torture me? Why?" She asked.

"I just have a feeling you are hiding something. I need to go." He interrupted her.

"Edwin please." She said softly.

"Cheri please be honest. Is she my daughter? You telling the truth will stop all of this. If she is mine, you allowing me to see her will help me." He retorted without regard for her feelings. "I have never known you to beg for a thing. So, what are you covering up now?"

"I just want you to stop please." Cheri asked again.

As she said this Kerry, who she thought was sleep, stepped quietly into the room next to the one she was in. He noticed that she had slipped out of bed. She had made a habit of it. At first, he thought she was checking on the baby.

"No. You be honest. Finally. About us. About this baby. About our future." Edwin replied to her.

Cheri sighed. "I am done. I mean it. I am done."

"What does that mean?" Edwin asked her.

"Just what I said. You have to go right?" She hung up in Edwin's face.

"Who is that?"

Cheri jumped out of her skin. "It is Gina. What are you doing up?"

"What were you guys talking about?" Kerry further inquired. "What are you done with?"

"Can I have a private moment with my sister?" Cheri said to throw him off.

"Not if I don't believe it is your sister," said Kerry.

"What do you mean? Who do you think it is?" Cheri asked.

"That is why I am asking you." Kerry retorted.

Cheri stormed away. She was caught on the wrong side between two men. It overwhelmed her. She also had no definite answers for her fiancé. Her only alternative was anger or hysterical crying.

Kerry did not like the suspicions he had about his fiancé. She had been acting strange since she returned to Texas. Knowing now she had a decent family and background; her behavior made no sense. He tried to push small things out his mind.

The big things threatened to push him over the edge. He knew pushing the issue with Cheri would bring him no new information. He decided to go back to bed. The person he wanted to talk to was sleep anyway.

The next day, he called his mom as soon as he arrived at work. He was sure something was going on with Cheri. He just could not prove it. His mom always had a balanced solution to his problems.

"Hey mom." He said quietly.

"Awe. What is wrong son?" She asked hearing his tone.

"Nothing I just need to ask you something." He answered.

"Go ahead." She said.

"Last night I caught Cheri whispering with someone on the phone. She told them she was done. When I asked her done with what, she would not answer." He sighed

"Well what do you mean would not answer?" His mom needed more information. "Who was she talking to?"

"She claims her sister. She walked away when I started asking questions." He said.

"Well, you do not have much to be honest. Just wait. If there is something going on, it will come out." She tried to encourage her son.

"Ok mom." That was not the answer Kerry was looking for.

"You do not need to stress where you do not have permanent evidence. Do not let your suspicions set you back? You hear me?" She continued.

"Ok mom, I will let you know it anything else happens. I have to get a little work done while I am here." Kerry said hanging up on his mom.

"That is fine. Make sure you call if you need to talk. I am here for you." His mom added.

"Thanks mom. I appreciate it." Kerry said lastly.

He figured his mom had a point. He still had a strong suspicion. He decided to take his mother's advice and wait. There was not much he could do without solid evidence.

On the other side of the country. Someone did have evidence. That someone was Edwin's wife. The scare he was using to scare Cheri ended up tripping him up to.

Some of the court documents were routed to the house instead of his office. As if wife sifted through the mail, she thought it was odd court documents were coming to the house. No one was going through a legal process at their address. Or so she thought.

Once she opened the documents, she only had to scan to see what they were for. In a few days, her husband would be appearing for parental rights of a female child. She was livid. She wanted answers.

"What is this?" Edwin's wife said slamming the documents down on his office desk.

"What are you doing here?" Edwin was stunned. His wife had just popped up at his job.

"What is this?" She asked again ignoring his question. She pointed to the court documents.

Edwin scanned the paperwork. "Can we go outside or drive around the corner?"

"What is this!" His wife demanded raising her voice.

"You see what it is, obviously you read it. Do not do this here." Edwin warned her.

"I cannot believe you have done this to me!" His wife screamed even louder.

"Look go home. We can discuss this later. Regardless of how upset you are, this establishment pays our bills. Respect that." Edwin was trying to route her to her car.

"You are low down and filthy. I hate you."
She yelled toward him.

"I know, I will see you when I get home."
Edwin said as he put her in the car.

He decided to cut that day short. He was not
sure what all his wife knew. He thought it was in his
best interest to find out. She was pretty mad.

At that very moment, he wished he would
have left the situation alone. Cheri asked him to go
away multiple times. He just could not let it rest.
Now he would dead the situation if he could.

By the time he had reached his house, his
fiancé was there waiting for him. She was still
upset. She began yelling and throwing things as
soon as he entered his home.

"How could you do this?" Was her first
question.

"I am sorry, I just-" Edwin had to dodge a
remote that was thrown towards his head.

"Shut up. You love her, don't you? I finally
have the courage to ask!" His wife yelled.

"No, I love you. I love our family. Please,
calm down." Edwin begged.

"You brought another child into our marriage!" He wife said crying.

"That is not set in stone. It might not be my child." Edwin said hoping to soothe the circumstance.

The whole time Edwin wished he was Edith's dad. To see the pain it brought to his wife's face, he wanted to take it all back. He all of a sudden wanted to drop the petition. He no longer wanted to know.

Unlike Edwin, Cheri was able to appear without her fiancé finding out. She simply said she was visiting her family in Texas. Which she was. She was just also going to test the paternity of her daughter.

Cheri appeared alone to address her case. Edwin was accompanied by his wife and lawyer. It was a very awkward moment. Cheri had never seen her before.

Edwin had preferred his wife did not show up. She was not fond of going herself. She just wanted to monitor the interactions between Edwin and Cheri. She did not get much from them.

They had spent the preceding month quarreling. They were not happy to see each other. Edwin did want to request to see the child. He just did not want to offend his wife since they were not sure.

The judge ordered the DNA test after both sides presented. During and after the hearing, he made sure not to make eye contact with Cheri. He knew his wife was watching. He was relieved he would know the truth. He was devastated how his wife found out.

They all knew the DNA test results would take time to come back. There were no pleasant goodbyes. There were no safe trip wishes. Everyone departed as separately as they came. At that point everyone was wishing it was not Edwin's baby.

"What are you going to do if she is yours?" Edwin's wife asked on the way home.

"I don't know. I will cross that bridge when I get there." He said quietly.

"What do you expect me to do if she is yours?" She continued to ask.

"Honestly I don't know. Do what is best for you I guess." He was not in the mood to talk.

"Did you think about your son? How he would be affected?" She was starting to get frustrated.

"How many times can I say I am sorry?" Edwin asked her.

"One thousand a day until those results come back." She said towards him.

He did not reply. He knew he was wrong. No matter what he said, it would not rectify what he did. Especially not at the moment.

Cheri and the baby returned to New York the day after the DNA swab. She stayed in communication with Kerry for the duration of her trip. As far as she could tell, he had no clue what was going home. That made it a relief to make it back home to him.

She had her sister pick her and the baby up from the airport. She knew Kerry would be at work once she landed. Plus, it would be good to catch up with her sister. She had not seen her since the last family holiday.

"Thank you so much for picking us up!" Cheri said as they pulled up in front of her home.

"No problem love. Let me help you. Just get the baby in the house. I will start with the luggage." Julia told her sister.

Cheri did as she was told. She was excited about being back home. She was grateful for her sister's help. She had no time to argue.

When she opens her front door, something was off to her. Not bad, but off. She asked her sister to stand with the baby while she checked the house. Kerry should have been at work, but there was a tv going.

She went towards their bedroom. The sound of the tv grew louder as she got nearer. Their door was only slightly open. Without opening the door, she could see Kerry fidgeting with a rolled up hundred-dollar bill.

He jumped when she decided to enter the room. She was only going to question why he was not working. But she saw a couple lines of white powder on his nightstand. That drew her attention from his job. They had a bigger problem.

"Julia, I know this is weird. Can you take the baby with you?" Cheri asked her sister.

"Everything ok? Sure, I love my niece." Julia asked concerned.

"No. It is not. That is why I need you to take her. Take her plane bags. They are supplied up." Cheri said helping her pack the baby back into the car.

Cheri thanked her sister again. Her sister assured her she was glad to help her sister. Cheri kissed Edith. She was not sure if she would see her baby the rest of the night.

Chapter 10: A Couple of Lines

"So? How did everything go?" Nathan asked Edwin.

"Man. I told you my wife found out right?" Edwin wondered.

"Yes. You also told me she demanded to escort you to court. That is why I am calling you my brother." Nathan chuckled.

"Sympathy would be nice man. It has gotten pretty bad between us. I am wondering if I should have even pursued this. Cheri is still contending the baby is not mine. I thought the pressure would make her tell the truth." Edwin said upset with himself.

"Well I think you did an upstanding thing. It was not the right thing overall. But you are trying to fix it. How was it with both your females in the same room? A court room at that." Nathan continued.

"You know, that is just it. That was my mistake. My wife was not ok, but consolable, before we appeared in court. She was even fine a few days after." Edwin went silent.

"You alright man?" Nathan became concerned.

"Man, she left." Edwin began to sob silently.

"Who. Your wife?" Nathan still probed.

Edwin was still silent for a second. "Yes. She left me and the baby. Told me to call her if my whores child turned out not to be mine." He paused again. "Funny thing is I married my whore. The lady I am dragging to court should have been my wife."

"Wow." Was all Nathan could manage to say.

"Yea I know." Edwin retorted.

Nathan felt bad for his brother. He also knew the role his brother had played in is own misery. He wanted to really console him. However, he felt his brother was only seeing the consequences of his actions.

Edwin was not the only one plagued by their harvest. Cheri had an issue of her own as well. After finding Kerry using drugs, she ended up moving in with her sister. She was not sure she wanted to leave Kerry. She was positive she would not accept his drug habit.

That was not the first time she caught him. Early in their relationship she found heroin in his car. She found out what is was because she almost threw it away. Kerry's reaction led to further investigation of the substance.

Her gut told her to call Edwin. She always called on him when things were not going right for her. Her pride served as a brick wall between she and him. She was still upset that he had summoned her to court.

Part of her wanted the baby to be Kerry's just to spite Edwin. Then again, Kerry had a drug problem. She loved him so much she hoped he would seek the appropriate help. He was a great father to Edith.

"Thank you again sister." Cheri reiterated as she joined her sister for a movie.

"Little baby sleep?" Julia said before starting the movie.

"Yes indeed. Thank so much for your help. Kerry does so much for her. I could not imagine being alone right now." Cheri said relieved.

"Child please. You are my sister and that is my niece. Speaking of, what is going on?" Julia poked.

Cheri sighed. "Look you have to keep this between us."

"Who will I tell?" Julia laughed.

"Your mom and all of your sister. You will forget I told you and retell it it me." They both fell out laughing.

There was an awkward pause after the laughter had died down. Cheri made a great joke, that is no doubt. They both knew Julia was waiting on her to finish.

Cheri sighed again. "I walked in ok Kerry doing drugs when we got home. I did not know exactly what I was going to do. That is why I asked you to take the baby."

Julia was blown away.

Cheri continued. "We fought pretty bad. I should have left with you because he was high when we arrived." She began to sob.

Julia went to embrace her sister. She retrieved tissues from her bathroom. She turned the lights on. It was clear the movie would be postponed.

"This is not the first time. I do not want to go into detail." Cheri tried to continue.

"Has he ever hit you?" Julia interrupted.

Cheri sobbed harder. Julia began to cry with her sister as well.

"Look, he is not perfect. I have my faults too." Cheri added.

"You sound like a victim." Julia had not tolerance for what her sister was going through. "Are you going back to him? You stay here for as long as you need too."

"No. I will eventually go home." Cheri said sadly.

"What! You said he has hit you. He has drugs in your home. Are you under a spell?" Julia was becoming irritated.

"Julia, I really need you to stand down. Let me take care of my family." Cheri was becoming frustrated herself. "You guys wonder why I keep to myself. You are so judgmental. I am going to bed."

The next few days between Julia and Cheri were quiet. Cheri wanted to go home, but her sister was actually right. However, she and Kerry had planned a life together. Cheri also felt Kerry's good outweighed his faults. She planned to stick to that plan.

When Kerry called to apologize, she was still apprehensive about going home. She at least wanted them to have a plan for his habit moving forward if she went back. She thought he had kicked it before. Here it was back again.

"How are you?" Kerry asked nervously.

"I am doing bad. Really bad because of what we are going through." Cheri was flat out honest.

"What can I do to make it better?" Kerry inquired.

"You problem solve. You created the issue. I will not suffer through the hurt and orchestrating the reconciliation. You did this." Cheri was firm.

"I understand. Can you guys come home so that I can start to reconcile?" Kerry wasted no time.

"Me coming home cannot be where your plan starts. It needs to start with a change in yourself." She wanted him to do more than just hope to stop.

"Like what? I just got stressed. And I made a wrong turn." Kerry pleaded.

"How many wrong turns do you have. Especially down that path? I cannot be associated with that." Cheri became upset.

"I do not want to argue baby. Please come home I will do whatever it takes." Kerry continued.

"Kerry you need to get some help. I cannot have my baby around that either." Cheri was stern.

"What do you mean. I cannot check myself in somewhere. Do you know where I work? I have to keep my reputation for us." Kerry said to her.

"Then you need to figure something out. The faster you figure it out, the sooner you will have your family back." Cheri said bluntly.

Kerry slammed down the phone. Cheri did not bother to call back. She meant what she had said. He had better put some hustle into it.

The results of the DNA test were returned while Julia was at her sister's house. The test had determined that Edwin was, in fact, the father of Edith. Cheri new the truth, still her stomach knotted up while she read the results. Edwin was actually shocked.

Cheri had denied his paternity so adamantly he thought he was mistaken. He also started to hope Edith was not his. He wanted to fix his own family. Things were unstable and it affected his child. His mother refused to see him until the results came back.

That made Edwin fear his wife's reaction. She had only been gone a couple of weeks. It felt like an eternity for Edwin. He had no help with his son most of the time. His parents helped when they could.

He formed a new appreciation for his wife. Looking back, he had hurt her often. As far as he knew, she had been loyal to him always. He grew sick thinking of telling her. However, he knew he had to tell her.

"Hey you." He said nervously.

"What do you want? Is the baby ok?" His wife asked with an irritated tone.

"Yes. I needed to talk to you." Edwin became nauseated.

"I do not have time." She said dismissively.

"The DNA results are here." Edwin paused. He lost the courage he had when he called her.

He knew the right thing to do was to tell her. He feared she really would leave them indefinitely if she found out Edith was his. He also did not want to bear the reaction of her pain.

"And?" She said after the pause became awkward.

Edwin sighed. "The little girl is not mine. I am sorry I did this to you."

"No you are not. You are sorry you got caught. We could have gone through this together if you were honest." She retorted.

138

"I just-" Edwin was interrupted.

"Do you still want Her?" She asked.

"No honey. I want you. I want my family." Edwin said sincerely. "Will you come back?"

"Come back for what? To be cheated on and humiliated. You think I do not know what you are doing? When I ask questions, you make me seem delirious. I was lucky to find the court documents. You would have covered that up too." His wife yelled. She was upset.

"You have every right to feel how you feel. I do not have any excuse for my actions. But I know you deserve more from me. We need you at home." Edwin went on.

"I do not know. You make me depressed and unsure of myself." She said softly.

"I am wrong for that. I am your husband. My job is to protect you and build you up. I know this was a rough one. I just want one more shot. I will not need another one honey." He tried to comfort her.

"Can I get that in writing?" She joked.

"How ever you need it from here on out." He assured her.

Edwin was able to reconcile with his wife. He realized he did not do it the right way. He just did not see a future fighting with Cheri over the baby. He decided to focus on the woman and child that he already had available to him.

Edwin indirectly gave Cheri the miracle she was looking for. She did not need the results to determine paternity for her. She was aware of who Edith's father was. She decided to wait for Edwin to make the first visitation demand. He had started this whole process anyway.

She decided to focus on Kerry and his sobriety. She knew her fiancé was not an addict. She wanted to keep it that way. She helped him find private counselors and support resources.

Edwin's disappearing act brought an era of peace for Kerry and Cheri's household. Once it seemed like they had made it past the mistakes, Kerry was more determined than ever to make Cheri his bride. Cheri finally agreed with him and they were able to set a date.

It appeared to Cheri that for some reason finding out about Edith brought an unexplainable peace. After a while she even wondered why Edwin went through the process to just disappear. Instead of determining why, she moved on with her life.

Chapter 11:
Balance

As Edith grew, so did Kerry and Cheri's happiness. The two eventually became a power couple in the city. Along with college buddies, they had plans to run the political sector of the city. They were on track too. Their first big plan was to get Kerry's best friend elected as the deputy mayor.

Kerry was doing so well for himself as a dentist, he wanted to open his own practice. He had a goal to own a franchise of dentistry facilities eventually. The extra success also made him think about their legacy. Cheri was doing well in law. They were not hurting for much.

"Cheri my love." Kerry asked her one morning over breakfast.

"Yes daddy?" She answered.

"I have a question. Can we sale this place?" He asked cautiously.

"What? Where ever will we live dear?" Cheri was puzzled.

"Well, I kind of bought you another house." He said smiling.

Cheri sat up in her seat. "Without me picking? Seriously? Thank you. Wait are you serious?"

"Yes I am serious. I want to take you and Edith to see it today." He said still smiling.

He was happy his wife stayed by his side. She had saw some of his darkest days. Every time, she helped him through it. He felt like buying her a house was the least he could do.

"Where is it?" Cheri was now inquisitive.

"Hmmm. About that. I kind of found a brownstone further from downtown." He paused for her response.

"Ok. But, why did you buy a house? A whole house? We can just rent this one unless you need the cash from the sale." She said calmly.

"No. We can rent it out for the cash flow." He paused. "I kind of wanted to ask can we expand our family?"

Cheri had to think about her own answer. She did not want to offend him. She was apprehensive about another baby for various reasons.

"So if I say no baby, will there be no house?" She asked shyly.

"Why would you say no baby?" He wanted more information.

"Everything is going so well. My career. Yours. I fear you being stressed out. That brings problems for both of us." She said hesitantly.

Kerry tapped his fork on his plate for a second. "Mama I will not relapse." Was all he said.

Cheri felt bad. She did not want to imply that in context to his parenting. The two never were a issue.

"I am not saying that." Was all she could manage to reply.

"Then what are you saying? We have one beautiful daughter already. I just want to try for another one. Look at our life. It is beautiful." He tried to keep the mood light.

Cheri instantly was stricken with guilt. His statement was touching, but far from true. She and Edwin had a beautiful daughter. Kerry was childless and did not know it.

"Ok daddy. How about we focus on one thing at a time. We can start with showing me the house. Get moved. Get tenants. Then make babies." She said to compensate for her own sin.

"I like the sound of that. You always give a me a route to my goals." He said thinking about having another baby. "Can I name this one too?"

"How far have you been thinking ahead sir? What if it is a boy? We cannot control the gender." Cheri said matter of factly.

"He would be Kerry Jr. of course. That is easy. I have an aunty her name is Judith. That was my second pick after I picked Edith." Kerry answered.

"Well there is a lot in between now and us making a baby. Let's go get dressed to see the house before your mom brings Edith back." Cheri suggested.

The more Kerry and his wife grew together, the more Edwin and his wife grew apart. Edwin did his best to keep his promise to his wife. He started being more faithful and committed to their marriage. They sought out counseling together.

Initially things seemed to work. His wife move back into their home. He made efforts it make her feel special. He set up date nights and tried to show he was invested in their relationship.

As time moved on things still eroded. His wife was very avid about acknowledging his efforts. She was very appreciative. She just had a tough time moving past their past. She had a tough time believing his honesty. She thought he was being honest before and he was not.

She also found it hard to believe Edwin did not still love Cheri. Edwin told her the results. Edwin never produced the results for her to see for herself. That made her feel uneasy.

After a while she was totally disconnected from Edwin. She began entertaining and flirting with other men. She felt she would have the same regard Edwin had for their marriage. That was little.

"He uh, who is this?" Edwin asked her one day as she was leaving the shower.

"What?" She asked innocently.

Edwin shoved her phone in her face. "Some guy is calling and looking for you!" He said pointing to an unsaved number.

She walked away from him without answering. Part of her was glad he found out. She wanted him to hurt the way she had.

"Excuse me. Who is this?" Edwin was trying not to lose his cool as he walked behind her.

"I don't know." She said with a smirk.

"You keep playing games." Edwin said and turned to storm away. He threw her cell phone against the wall.

He went to call Nathan. The past few months had been that way for them. He was not sure how much more he could take. He just did not want to be the reason his son grew up in a broken home. He worked hard to fix his wrongs.

"Hey man, you busy?" Edwin asked as his brother picked up the phone.

"Uh, go ahead what is wrong brother?" Nathan said in response.

"Man, it is getting hard for me. It seems like the more I try, the more she pushes me away." Edwin said exhausted.

"Well, you are dealing with a scorned woman. I tell you the same thing all the time. Work it out or move around. But do not rehearse the same issues." Nathan suggested.

"I hear you. I just feel like I owe it to her to work it out. The more I work. The more she throws it back on my face. I think she is cheating on me." Edwin said and his voice cracked.

"Why do you think that?" Nathan wanted to know more.

"I intercepted a call today while she was showering. The guy was not aware she was married. He told me to ask her who he was." Edwin sounded devastated.

"You might be onto something brother. Now what? She stops cheating or you walk? You want for her to finish cheating like she waited for you?" Nathan asked seriously.

"That last option sounded insane." Was all Edwin could reply.

"Well come up to New York to take your mind off things for a while. Bring my nephew." Nathan offered.

"You can have that state brother. I do not want any parts of New York. I have my own problems here." Edwin went silent.

"Well brother I will call you after I close up tonight. We are busy, but I always have time for you." Nathan said ended the call.

Edwin could only think of Edith after he hung up. He had a handsome son at home. He still wondered about his daughter in New York. He asked about her undetectable through mutual friends. He heard his daughter had a fine life.

When he flirted with thoughts of seeing her. He was always paralyzed by the fear of messing up her life. He heard Cheri and her husband were doing very well for themselves. He did not want to interrupt Edith's life with he and his wife's drama.

150

He vowed to meet her one day. He just wanted to wait until she was an age she could understand his stance. He also felt it was partially her mother's fault that things were the way they were. He did not want to interrupt their relationship.

It was not like he was ready to step in and make Edith's life better. His own was in shambles. He felt it was best to keep his distance for the sake of their family unit. It seemed to be everything he would have wanted to give to his child. Surely it was better than the toxic atmosphere he and his wife created.

Despite their troubles, Edwin had a little more fight in him. He wanted to fight for his son to have a stable family unit as well. He took responsibility for his wrong doing early on. He hoped that would buy him bit of happiness with his wife later on.

Book I
Excerpt

I was 17 when I realized my mom already knew my dad had a drug problem. I explained what I had witnessed in grave detail and shock. I was shook. There were whole school lesson on not "doing drugs", thanks to sober minds. Lessons that that resonate with generations.

She stood still as a statue as warm tears rolled down my face in the December storm outside. I explained to her that he was rocked back in his recliner, breathing, but unresponsive. As I called 911 I noticed a needle on it side table with a small glob of black goo. All I could think as the responder is asking me questions was "I wasn't supposed to be home".

I told my mom that the first responders rushed into our brownstone without regard. That was why the door frame was tethered. Her face never changed. Her stare never left me. She only blinked when I said "I".

I told her my relief when the paramedics were able to revive him. The possessed some potion, they shot it in him, he woke up. I apologized to her they would not let me in the ambulance because I was a minor. We were taught family first, I thought I had left him hanging. As I grew older, I realized he left us hanging.

When I finished my monologue, so full of zeal, concern, and defeat, she simply said,

"I am sorry baby."

She turned and walked away. I realized she knew. She knew because she did not react. My mom was a reactor. She was the ultimate reactor. Yet there was little response to what would be the most powerful shift in my life.

"Mom"

My mom did not break her glance from the front window, "Yes babe?"

"Are you going to see dad?" I hesitated because I was unsure of her emotions. I had never seen her like this.

She paused for what seemed like an eternity and said slowly, "No".

My mom was always up for questions, but as I said, she is a reactor. I chose my words carefully when I asked my next question. I considered her hurt after, I realized she knew. I did not want to further a painful cause.

"Mom, I will only ask one more question."

"Go ahead my love."

"What was type of dr-."

"It was heroin."

I could see a tear roll down her face through the window's reflection. I left her there to bear the weight of whatever emotion she was bearing. I did not want to. I wanted to hug her. I wanted her to hug me. I wanted to understand it all.

I retreated to my bedroom and shut the door. I collapsed into my bed and cried for a while. I cried for me. I cried for my mom. I cried for my little sister who would eventually come home to the somberness.

She was trapped at my aunt's house thanks to the storm. We were trapped at home. I cried a little harder. I walked through my front door celebrating I was able to make it home before the storm hit. I walked into my living room and discovered my unconscious father. My mom had told me to stay in safe at my best friend's house until it passed.

I cried a bit more. My mom always said I need to listen more. She says sometimes there is good reason to heed a good instruction. Today her words were as clear as the truth I witnessed. My father was a drug addict. I cried until sleep took it's turn in my life for the day.

Everything about the next morning said my life had changed. We were a pretty rambunctious family. I was used to waking up to someone's music, be it classical, gospel, or jazz. On weekdays, the aroma of an imported coffee bean brewing would tickle my nose as I woke.

If my mom woke me up, it was stern and militant. "Edith, Edith." Is all I will hear and I had about 5 seconds before the covers were ripped from my bed with a "Good Morning." Mom is the house timekeeper. She did not allow the morning pleasure of asking for more time in bed. When mom says something, it is almost always an imperative. Even "Good Morning."

When I was younger, I saw my mom drag an older cousin from the bed by an ankle. This happened after my mom said "Good Morning" twice. I thought it wise to always get up on the first one after that. That cousin still spent many nights in my home after that incident to my surprise.

If my dad woke me up things were different. He'd kiss you a few times. He would wiggle your nose or ear. You could smell his aftershave and toothpaste above the imported coffee beans. He was a lover. He would check on me and see what I needed.

After our talk, he would leave me to get dressed. He then would wake my sister. Her morning almost never went well. She was daddies baby girl. She almost never takes well to being woken up.

My mom and dad had a pact. He was responsible for waking her up and getting her ready every morning. This pact happened after my mom left her at home multiple times with my dad for "wasting her time". In plain English, my sister either pitched a royal fit or ran around the house until my mom was late. I think my mom would leave the Pope before being late.

This morning was cold. Cold because my dad had not switched the heater on after we slept. We slept with the house cool in the winters. My dad would wake up before everyone and warm the brownstone and start his routine.

My body was weak, but I crept to the thermostat. The heater began to roar almost immediately. I walked towards my parent room to check on my mom. The King size bed was empty when I arrived. So was the bedroom.

I began searching the house. I immediately became so anxious with negative thoughts I did not think to just call her name. I found her in the kitchen with her back to the opening. This was unusual. My mom always sat at the island facing the opening of the kitchen. It was her spot. She was sitting in my dad's chair.

Relieved to see her, I hugged her. She hugged me back, but her hug was different. My mom even hugged with authority. This morning her hug seemed to need me more than I needed it. I hugged her tighter. She let her body go limp in my arms.

My mom looked horrible. I mean that in the most loving way. She was a judge. I almost never saw a hair out if place on this women before 9 pm. I admired everything about my mom. She was who I wanted to be. This morning my hero was in need of saving.

There was no book, phone, or document in front her. There was no imported coffee brewing. This was different. We were allowed to sit with much ideal time. My mom had a "either you are researching or creating" rule. She said "the ideal mind was the devil's workshop". She modeled that very rule herself. My mom was always up to something. Today she was a cold statue in my father's chair.

My muscles were relaxing due to the brownstone warming up. I don't remember meeting my mom without caffeine. There was a strange woman in my kitchen wearing my mom's skin. She was creepy. I started brewing coffee in hopes of getting my mom back.

I grabbed her a blanket. She was shivering. I think my mom may have snapped. Before I could consider not having to healthy parents anymore, the coffee machines beeping broke my train of thought. I added her French Vanilla creamer and a drop of hazelnut extract to her cup of coffee.

It was my first time making her coffee. I had watched her do it a million times. My mom was not one to need much assistance. She was like the house warden. We were not concerned with her needs, we were busy meeting her expectations. But a warm and loving warden, if we were being loud or arriving late some where.

She watched the mug for a strange time. She picked it up slowly, blew it to cool it, and took a sip.

"Thank you baby girl."

"You are welcome mom."

She drank her coffee some more. She still hadn't relaxed. But she seemed a wee bit more alive. Which helped ease my anxiety.

"Mom."

"Yes."

"What or where, maybe I should ask how, can I contact dad."

"You can't access him right now."

"Why", I asked confused.

She put her coffee back on the island. She kept her state on her mug for another strange minute. I have never seen this woman lost for words. This has to be bad.

She looked at me. For the first time she to eye. The strange lady in front of me had no eye lashed or eye brows. A sure sign she had lost it. Her eye were more swollen than mine from crying over night I presumed. Yet she was still beautiful.

"Edith."

She paused for a very long time.

"Edith, your dad has been checked into a rehab." Her voice cracked while her lips formed the word rehab. "He will be in a state of detoxing, for a while. I will let you know when it was ok to speak with him." Her blood shot eye went back to her mug.

My mom's heart was broken. More broken than mine. I had more questions, as always, but I did not want to drag her through the hurt of yesterday. Or the days to come as so she has formed it.

The storm was still whistling outside. Not as loud as last night. It seemed to be subsiding. New York winters can be rough, but the view after it blankets out world with snow is beautiful. We were not going anywhere anytime soon.

I cut on my mom's favorite jazz record and played it on the brownstone speaker system. If we had to be here, we could at least relax. I started my day as if yesterday did not happen. A snow storm may close school, but it doesn't excuse you from the assignments.

I grabbed my backpack from my room and returned to the island. My mom was in the same spot. With the same cup. With the same stare. I hugged her again and sat down with her and began my studies.

My mom took a deep sigh. "Edith."

"Yes ma?"

"Do you remember the business trip your dad took about two years ago? He was "out of the country"," she said slowly.

"Yeah, Milan right? He brought us back some nice key chains and souvenir hats. A marketing conference." I responded.

"Your dad was never in Milan. He was in a Florida rehabilitation center."

Someone's cell phone began to buzz in the background almost instantaneously with the ending of her sentence. She asked me to retrieve her phone, in case it concerned my baby sister. As I walked to get the phone I thought about the lie my parents had told. I was recoiled at the length they went to cover it up. I wondered what else they had lied about.

It was indeed her phone. The call was from my aunt, my aunt that was housing my sister. My mom retreated to her office to speak with my aunt. It was located at the back of the house. It was understood if she went there, she needed privacy or quietness. It was her cave.

I tried to resume my studies, but her sentence had me distracted. I retrieved my own cell phone from my room. I had not checked it since I found my dad. There were tons of messages and social media notifications. Most of them from my boyfriend.

Drew was my first boyfriend and my current boyfriend. We started dating when we were 13. We broke up often and made up always. I'm sure he was worried I had not responded. Were hardly went a few hours without contacting each other.

His messages signaled his worry. I wanted to rush and call him back, but I had no words to say. My dad was a top dentist at a well-known practice in the city. I was forbade from telling my families closest secrets to an unforgiving world. My mom explained "it takes a million things to build a good reputation, and one thing to tear it down." So we kept our toughest times in house as a practice.

I sent him a text hoping he would not call, but he did. I ignored the call and told him we had a family emergency. I did not want to go through his series of questioning. I had enough on my mind. He could be quite a butt hole sometimes.

He replied with a few unhappy face emojis and told me to call him soon. I assured him I would then go straight to social media. I needed a distraction. I was careful not to like or comment on any social post. Drew would perceive it as time I could have used to talk to him.

As I scrolled, I still thought about my parents. Most of my timeline was littered with cliché snow day post. My friends were sledding and enjoying the day off. I was wondering how many more times my dad was on some camouflage business trip.

About the Author

Toy Taylor is a native of Waco, Tx. She currently manages a behavior unit in Austin, Tx. For more information and other works by the author please visit toytaylorbooks.com.

Other Books:

A Peace of Edith

Toy Taylor

Publish 5 Books in 5 Months or Less

I have many other books!
Check out my site: toytaylorbooks.com